FROM ISLAND TO ISLAND

FROM ISLAND TO ISLAND

RECOLLECTIONS ON OVER 50 YEARS
AS A BAHÁ'Í PIONEER TO THE CARIBBEAN

Chronicles from the Paccassi Pioneering Journeys to the Caribbean Islands of Puerto Rico, St. Thomas, Barbados, St. Vincent, Dominica, St. Lucia and Trinidad and Tobago from 12 October 1965 to Present, May 2020

BY PAT PACCASSI

FROM ISLAND TO ISLAND. Copyright © 2020 Patricia Paccassi. All rights reserved. Printed in the United States of America. No part of this book may be used or reproduced in any manner whatsoever without permission except in the case of brief quotations embodied in critical articles and reviews. For more information, contact Patricia Paccassi directly: paccassi@gmail.com

Cover and book design by Cheryl Watson Cooney

ISBN: 9798648680449

CONTENTS

CHAPTER 1: INTRODUCTION 1

CHAPTER 2: PUERTO RICO 4

CHAPTER 3: ST. THOMAS 13

CHAPTER 4: BARBADOS 30

CHAPTER 5: DOMINICA 63

CHAPTER 6: ST. LUCIA: 1ST STAY 68

CHAPTER 7: TRINIDAD AND TOBAGO 88

CHAPTER 8: ST. LUCIA: 2ND STAY 104

CHAPTER 9: STORIES 114

CHAPTER 10: CV OF BAHÁ'Í EXPERIENCES 126

| 1 |

INTRODUCTION: FEBRUARY 1964 – 1965

It is not often that one can look to a specific point and say, "That's when it all started", but in this case I can. I became a Bahá'í in February 1964 and Frank a few weeks later in Carmichael, California. Our spiritual Mother was Maxine Roth and our spiritual Father was Wayne Hoover.

It was a foot dragging process for me. But thank God, Maxine was a wonderful, persistent teacher. She remembered we had first met in 1963, during a volleyball game at the elementary school that both our children attended. After that game she said she went home, said prayers and was so sure of an answer she got, she immediately told her then non-Bahá'í husband, Marty, "the Paccassis will be Bahá'ís before next Riḍván!"

This is not the forum for the story of that long year to Riḍván 1964, but it is in the book about various pioneers "And the Trees Clap their Hands" by Clair Veer land, published by George Ronald Books.

Suffice it to say that during the Fast period in 1964, I enrolled and Frank right after me. Actually, he was ready much earlier, but he waited for me. The following year was one of great fun and lots of teaching, and one hopes, spiritual growth and weaning.

Maxine had wonderful firesides every week which were well attended and greatly looked forward to by me. One day I went to visit her and made a remark about the upcoming fireside and she told me I couldn't come! What? Why not? Well she said, "If you like firesides so much start your own". At that point, my underlying competitive, petty nature kicked in, and I replied, "Ok, but you can't come to mine either". Later I realized she was starting me on my own path of service to the Faith.

For the next several months we continued with the teaching and firesides. Ours was well attended also. Wayne Hoover, in spite of living in San Francisco, a hundred miles away, came on a regular basis to give the talks. I learned a very special message one night during one of his talks. One of the young seekers asked a question which Wayne began to answer. I was sitting in the middle of the room between the seeker and Wayne. As Wayne was answering the question, I became increasingly annoyed. He was not answering the question! I wasn't sure what to do, should I interrupt, keep still, talk to the seeker and/or Wayne later. Then I turned my head, and the seeker was nodding his head off, up and down, clearly saying yes, yes, yes! I then realized that often it is the unasked question that needs answering, and one must listen closely to hear it.

I mention these lessons learned as I have come to realize that it is these lessons which come all through life. If one cannot understand and be connected to the Holy Spirit during your life as a Bahá'í, whether a pioneer or not, all will not go smoothly. This applies especially as a pioneer living in a new culture. I have seen so many new pioneers not being able to adapt to a new culture simply because they looked at the wrong things in life, especially in a new cultural life. When I heard negative remarks about the place, area, people, conditions etc. I knew it wouldn't be long before they were gone!

A good example of cultural unawareness came from a pioneer who had recently come from the United States as a pioneer to Barbados and was a strong administrative type. Phil Wood who was the chairman of the National Spiritual Assembly was talking at a meeting about our Local Spiritual Assemblies. When our new pioneer heard that there were only ten Local Spiritual Assemblies on Barbados, he stood up exclaiming "Good God man, how does your National Assembly function?" Phil, without skipping a beat, put his hands up in the air, clenched his fists and said, "We hang on real tight!"

But back to 1964 as new Bahá'ís. It passed wonderfully! Then in April 1965, The Riḍván Message contained a message from the Hands of the Cause of God, including this quote from Shoghi Effendi on the need for pioneers:

> *"There is no time to lose. There is no room left for vacillation. Multitudes hunger for the Bread of Life. The stage is set. The firm and irrevocable Promise is given. God's own Plan has been set in motion.... The powers of heaven and earth mysteriously assist in its execution.... Let the doubter arise and himself verify the truth of such assertions. To try, to persevere, is to ensure ultimate and complete victory."*

Shoghi Effendi, Messages to America, p. 17

The seed was planted!

| 2 |

PUERTO RICO:
OCTOBER 1965 - JULY 1966

That quote from the Guardian hit me right away; accepting challenges was a way of life for me and from that quote came the conviction to pioneer! As for Frank, moving, especially for the Faith was no problem. We began the process of writing letters and sending out Frank's resumes all over the world. Unlike missionaries who are paid by their church, Bahá'í pioneers go and maintain themselves. This in itself helps one to be more a part of the new environment. So Frank's resumes went out and we waited and waited and waited.

I also began to have second thoughts. As a result of her early arrival on the planet, our youngest daughter, Judy, was in special education. What would happen to her education? My maternal Grandma Snyder came to live with us from Detroit, Michigan in 1964. She had become a Bahá'í here on her 80th birthday, but she was a lot younger than her years. She was active, lively, gregarious and with an inquiring mind. How would she react to living overseas? I had just started back to college to get my degree. Should I give this up, after all, education in the Bahá'í Faith is highly commendable. As we were actively teaching and working for the Faith in Sacramento, perhaps these reasons were enough to stay here.

In addition, the Foreign Goals Committee who were responsible for sending pioneers to Bahá'í goal areas stressed that we should not go anywhere without a job! And no one had answered our letters.

One other consideration was that we had not specifically asked Grandma if she wanted to go. We offered to her that we would see that she was well cared for in the States if she didn't want to go with us, but she said she would like to go and things then began to fall into place for us.

A definitive answer came quickly and decisively one night after a fireside. Frank, who was normally easy going, and says things such as "Whatever you want to do is ok with me" surprised me when he announced firmly "Tomorrow I am going into work, resign and we are going pioneering!" People who were there told me I went pale, I know I felt weak. But that was it. We were on our way. As Bahá'u'lláh says the best provision for one's journey is trust in God.

We finally decided to go to Puerto Rico. It had many industries and Frank with his engineering experience should be able to get work. Ignoring the fact that they spoke Spanish and we did not, we put our house on the market, packed up and shipped our goods to Puerto Rico.

On the 12 October 1965, we arrived in San Juan, Puerto Rico as pioneers. It was a year and a half after we had become Bahá'ís. We were, Momma, Poppa, two young daughters, Lynn, age 11, and Judy, age 9, and my maternal Grandmother, Elsie Snyder, age 81, oh, and, a registered French Poodle named Robbie. Robbie had been a gift from a friend who said he would generate income for us as he was a pure-bred poodle.

We had picked Puerto Rico as a post after a prolonged consultation with Foreign Goals, but they were not enthusiastic about our going anywhere without a job. Frank had a BS in Physics and had been working as an engineer in the Polaris Missile Program in California and there was a company in Puerto Rico which we thought would hire him. He had written everywhere else without any responses. We finally had to just go to this island which had been suggested by Foreign Goals. Then they realized that job or no job, we were going pioneering. The only thing left for us to do was to go and pray that it was the right thing to do!

We had originally planned to go pioneering with four other Bahá'í families, the Roths, Leebs, Fannings and the Mortensens. We were all Bahá'ís in our Carmichael, California community and great friends. This however did not materialize, so we ended up going by ourselves the next year. All the other three families did become pioneers at a later time, just not in a clump.

We were picked up at the San Juan airport by another pioneer family, the Heaths. We didn't know who was going to meet us. As I watched people go by me, a stream of young, blonde, light coffee-coloured beautiful children and their mother passed by and I thought this is them! And sure enough it was! This was my first experience, but not the last with recognizing someone without ever having seen them before. They immediately put us a DC-3 plane to the other side of the island to a small town called Ponce. To give you an idea of size and comfort of the plane, we could hear Robbie, the dog, barking loudly in the luggage space all the way!

I can still remember our first night in Ponce. It was unbelievably hot and muggy, all six of us in a hotel room, trying to go to sleep, hearing people chatter in a language none of us knew, and me thinking of the old joke "What's a nice girl like me doing in a place like this!"

We were staying in a hotel which was very close to an amazing old Fire House. I found out later it is now a Historic Registered Landmark and is currently a Museum.

It didn't take long to know we had to get out of the hotel and find another place to live. After family consultation, it also was realized we were going to need a car of some kind. So after saying lots of prayers, off we went. Reality began to set in as lot after car lot was selling cars starting at eight or nine hundred dollars, way beyond our present means. We came to another lot and heard the same story. So Frank asked if he didn't have anything cheaper. The man scratched his head and said, "Well I have one back here". He took us way back, and there sat this dusty, rusty, multi-coloured car looking as if it would have to be pushed off the lot. The man said, "You can have this for one hundred and fifty". Now Frank is really startled as we had been quoted prices much higher, so he says loudly "What". The man who is now startled says, "OK, Ok, you can have it for seventy-five dollars." Frank is now speechless, so I poke him in the side and quietly say "That's what we said prayers for". We now have a bargain. As the man shows us the car, he goes back to his office, gets his screwdriver, and opens the trunk and points to a spare tire even shinier than those on the car.

We later called her Baby, as she really did need to be treated as such. For example, she had a cranky carburetor. It would stop working whenever and wherever it wished. Frank always fixed it by taking it apart and putting it back together. The transmission gears would snap out of place regularly. Frank would reach through a hole under the front seat, snap them back into place and away we go. The engine overheated very often, so we would park, find the nearest coffee shop, sit for a while, go back to the car, and take off.

Also. whenever it rained our passengers in the back seat would get sprayed through a hole in the floor when we went over a puddle.

The one idiosyncrasy of the car that was not at all endearing to me was that she did not like to carry her passengers up a steep hill. So, at the bottom of a hill, all passengers disembarked while she and the driver went up the hill and waited until we could join them. But she lasted the whole nine months we were there. Iris, one of the new Bahá'ís, against our better judgment, bought Baby for seventy-five dollars. She drove it home from our departure at the airport and parked it by her Grandmother's house. When Iris went back to get it her grandmother said, "But Iris, I gave it to the man who said he was getting it for you." Oh my, Oh well, probably just as well.

If I ever write a book, I most certainly will have to include a chapter called "The Car". I have talked to lots and lots of pioneers who have these great funny stories about their cars. My son-in-law, Richard Berry, tells of picking up Hand of the Cause of God Dr. Muhájir at the airport in Grenada in a car belonging to another pioneer, Arthur Winner, whose car was surely was a descendant of the one we had in Puerto Rico.

Let Rick tell his story:

"...Arthur's car, an English Ford, ran, but you didn't dare turn it off if you were planning on using further that day. The generator didn't work, and the battery was weak. To start the car, Arthur rolled the car down our common driveway. He also always made sure he parked on a hill.

We got to the airport, about an hours' drive from our house, about five minutes before the plane was due to arrive. Arthur thought it would be OK to leave the car running for that short a time. Of course, the plane was delayed. About an hour as I remember. Then Dr. Muhájir finally arrived, got through customs, and after sufficient hugs and greetings we all three walked out to the car park. The car had stopped running! We loaded the luggage in the car and told Dr. Muhájir to just stand by the side of the road while I pushed the car and Arthur would come back and get us both. He said OK. I started pushing the car, and after a few feet noticed it suddenly became much easier than I had expected. Dr. Muhájir had joined the car push. Both Arthur and I said "No, Dr. Muhájir just wait and we will get it started." Of course he kept pushing and the car was soon started.

We all got in the car. Arthur and I were both profusely apologizing for having to have the car push-started. Dr. Muhájir smiled and laughed and said 'My dears it's alright. Every pioneer has the same car'."

We had moved from our Puerto Rican hotel to a new and almost completed apartment complex. It was clean, plenty of room, with four bedrooms and not expensive. We had finally realized that most Puerto Ricans speak English when they choose to. Our first night I went to bed, snuggling down for a good night's sleep, only to discover one of the reasons the rent was so reasonable. There was a chicken farm about 10 feet from our bedroom. Now contrary to the urban U.S. opinion that roosters only crow at dawn, I am here, testifying to the falseness of that belief! They crow on and off all night and all day long. Welcome to the Caribbean, our culture shock had begun!

In a short time we were joined by another American pioneer, Leonard Ericks. He was young, handsome, and an artist. His story of how he came to pioneer is fun, as are most similar stories. He lived in Los Angeles, California and wanted to be an actor. His studies included all the things young aspiring actors need to do; singing, dancing, horseback riding, diction, etc. He had been invited to a fireside by a friend and though attracted, felt this could certainly not include him. However it wasn't too long before he found himself writing a letter expressing his desire to pioneer. The only problem was that he couldn't make himself mail it. He'd walk up to a mailbox and couldn't drop it in. Then, one time, much to his own surprise, he snatched the mailbox door open and in went the letter! Now he was here in Puerto Rico. He did end up getting a job in one of the large department stores as a decorator. He has remained a pioneer all of his life!

The Bahá'í Community in Puerto Rico seemed quite large to me at that time, very friendly and open to newcomers. I had enrolled in a class in Spanish soon after we got there, but I was struggling with the language. A Catholic University near us was holding Spanish lessons designed to train their missionaries to go into South America. Worked for me and I enrolled. I was 37 at that time, and languages are best learned at a young age. But the Bahá'ís were patient and supporting in my efforts to learn Spanish. I remember one large meeting, where Jose Monge was the chairman. After a long introduction in Spanish, he leaned over to where he could see me and said in English, "You got that Pat?" I, of course answered, not totally truthful, "Si, Si".

It was here that we found our first spiritual children. A long-time pioneer to Mayaguez, Puerto Rico, Dorothy Behar, used to visit us on a regular basis as we had become good friends. It was around Christmas time, and one could

hear carols from every direction. Iris Guinals de Maul, one of the young women from upstairs, came down and wanted to know if we knew all the words to the song, "The Twelve Days of Christmas?" You bet we would try!

As the weeks went by, we all became good friends, and the talk of Faith started. Iris liked what she heard, but she was a law student at the university across the street plus she did not want to take this kind of step without first talking to her husband who was in the US Armed Forces at that time.

Also during this time frame, a young man, Noel Robbles y Robbles started coming to visit. He seemed attracted right from the start. I can still see him going home late one night, reading a Bahá'í book stopping under streetlights to be able to read the book better. After a few visits and more reading, he declared himself as a Bahá'í.

Iris, however, was not showing that kind of interest in spite of all the discussions we had about the Faith. In the early part of the year 1966, late one night, when she was trying to study, she came downstairs all distraught! She said she has started to pray and looked up into the sky and saw the stars formed in a symbolic shape that she recognized as meaning that the Bahá'í Faith was true, and that she needed to join!

The ensuing events in Iris's life showed her becoming a dedicated, devoted Bahá'í. She was elected to the first National Spiritual Assembly of the Bahá'ís of Puerto Rico. She also was the first Puerto Rican to go on Pilgrimage. Her other services include travel teaching to Caribbean Islands.

Here is our group in Ponce: L to R standing: Noel, Leonard Ericks (holding Robbie), Dorothy Behar, Pat; Kneeling: Frank, Lynn, Iris Guinals de Maul, Judy

Noel, however, soon moved to New York, and

PUERTO RICO | 11

we have not had any contact with him since.

It was here in Puerto Rico that I learned that pioneers come in all sizes, shapes and descriptions. One should always keep an open mind and not doubt the guidance another receives from Baha'u'llah. We met Vivian Taylor, a pioneer from the United States. She told us the way she had decided to come here. She was sitting one day, wanting to go pioneering somewhere, and as she sat looking at the sky and the clouds, one passed by that she says was in the shape of Puerto Rico, and that was it for her. Here she is in Puerto Rico, happy and serving.

Vivian was in her 30's, tall, slim, very blonde and clearly beautiful. She later left Puerto Rico, staying in our islands, from St. Thomas to Antigua. She served the Faith, devotedly, and steadfastly, passing away in Antigua, having married Counsellor Rowland Estall years before. I loved that lady.

Our highest priority in order to stay was for Frank to get a job. Frank was hired within a month, as a local, at CORCO, the petrochemical plant outside Ponce. This meant he received 60% of the salary of those hired from overseas. But the job didn't last long.

One of the ground rules at the petrochemical plant was religion was not to be discussed. The secretary of Frank's big boss asked him a question about the Faith, so she was given a pamphlet. Nothing more was said.

However, Frank was accused of telling people about the Faith. When it was mentioned that it was his secretary who asked, Frank was accused of trying to blame the secretary and was fired. That was in May 1966.

I am sure there were other factors involved. As pioneers we wanted to be near and associate with Puerto Ricans. We moved to an area far from the "American Ghetto" where all the Continentals from the United States lived. I had also started taking Spanish lessons, and it was preferred by the company that its engineers speak English. We sent Lynn to a public school, knowing she would pick up Spanish quickly. None of our moves made a good impression on Frank's boss. But also, as I learned slowly, but surely, Bahá'u'lláh has his own plan. It is His Plan that we want to follow, and hope that we are.

After he lost his job in May, the family moved to a suburb of the capital, San Juan, where Frank began looking for a job. The house we moved to was one I will never forget! We were shown the outside and it looked fine. Moving inside, the rooms were large and cool, with enough bedrooms and the rent not too expensive. AND then we opened the door to the bathroom. No telling how long the house had been vacant. Leaning against the wall in the bathtub was an old mop, AND the room was totally, completely, covered with brown shiny-winged roaches two to three inches long. We could not believe our eyes, and jumped back. The land lady said, casually, "Oh I'll spray and get rid of those for you". Welcome to the tropics!

Another job however, did not materialize. I now had to write Foreign Goals, with a sheepish "It looks like you were right after all, we should have gotten a job first, and it looks as though we will have to return to the United States". In a few weeks we got a letter back telling us that as we are already in the area see if Frank can get a job in St. Thomas. They will be forming a new National Spiritual Assembly in the Leeward, Windward and Virgin Islands. They can use some more help.

We scraped together the funds and Frank booked a flight to St. Thomas.

| 3 |

ST. THOMAS:
JULY 1966 – OCTOBER 1971

Frank's description of this move from Puerto Rico to here follows. It should be noted that this rendering of Frank's was done by him in the third person.

"A regional National Spiritual Assembly of the Leeward, Windward and Virgin Islands was due to be formed at Riḍván 1967, with its seat in Charlotte Amalie, St. Thomas.

It was suggested that Frank contact Katherine Meyer, a Knight of Bahá'u'lláh for Margarita Island who was secretary of the Local Spiritual Assembly in St. Thomas to see if she knew of any jobs that were available in St. Thomas. A quick trip there, a phone call, an interview and Frank had a job in the office of a small construction outfit.

Dorothy Behar came to St. Thomas with the Paccassis. We were able to find a house large enough for all of us. It was just around the corner from long time pioneers, the Harmers, Marjorie and Ellerton and their three children Susie, Michele and Tony.

Most of the work done by the construction company was for the Virgin Island Government and the local phone company. They did other work like redoing an old rum storage warehouse that had been just opened after many years of wrangling in the courts. The boss kept the five 55-gallon barrels of rum from the warehouse that was supposed to be dumped. Frank commented on the irregularity of that to them on that and was ignored.

About five weeks after Frank had been hired, a duplicate check on another matter for several thousand dollars was received from the government. This was a duplicate payment that they had already received. The boss decided to keep it instead of returning it. It was suggested by Frank that if the check was returned the Government would look at them in a much more favorable light. The boss not only didn't see it that way, instead, he decided to fire Frank.

In reality, St. Thomas was not an easy place to obtain work, especially for a Continental, that is, someone from the U.S. mainland. In August 1966, a one-day tryout job for Frank with a local surveyor gave him such a very bad case of hay fever that his nose was stuffed up for several years to come.

Frank scoured the island of St. Thomas but could not find a job. The money was weeping away. Pat decided, resultantly, that she had to go to work. She found a job at Spencely's jewelry store. To her surprise, she was good at it.

By December 1966 Frank was working at the Welfare Department as the Director of Welfare Research and Statistics. He promptly posted on the wall the nine Baha'i holidays when work is suspended.

The job at times sent him to the U.S. regional Welfare office in Charlottesville, Virginia. On these trips he had the great pleasure of meeting with the Chutes. One of Rúhíyyih Khánum's cousins was Jean Chute.

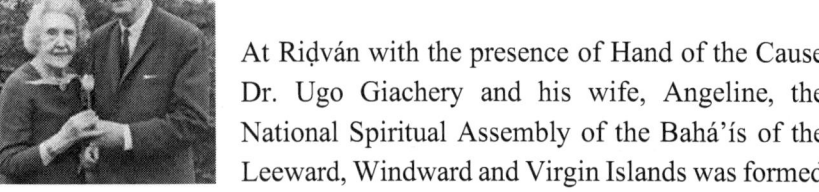

At Riḍván with the presence of Hand of the Cause Dr. Ugo Giachery and his wife, Angeline, the National Spiritual Assembly of the Bahá'ís of the Leeward, Windward and Virgin Islands was formed with its seat in St. Thomas."

Our good friend Dorothy Behar, another pioneer in Puerto Rico, decided to go with us to St. Thomas. So we once again packed up and moved. I didn't know at the time that this was to be only the second in a series of moves throughout the Caribbean for the Faith. Much later I recalled when we were first new Bahá'ís in Carmichael, California, the Local Spiritual Assembly asked us to move to help a nearby community, which was even nearer to Franks' work. I said, "No, I'm not moving that far". Oh my, had I known!

It was here in St. Thomas that a letter from the Universal House of Justice arrived in the latter part of 1960's. In it was the appeal for pioneers to remain at their posts. This, then, was when I decided that we would not, ever, return to the United States, but would remain at our post.

During the first few months we lived in St. Thomas, I learned a basic principle that Bahá'u'lláh has always applied to us as pioneers. Frank was not yet able to get another job in St. Thomas. Our funds had dwindled down, even with me working, so that at the end of the month, we did not have enough money to pay the rent and buy groceries. One day a few weeks later we got a letter in the mail from Maxine and Marty Roth who were minding our house in Carmichael, California that we had not been able to sell before we left the States. In it was a check with enough to pay the rent that month, with $100 left over. YAY! It seems that there had been a hit and run driver who ran into our garage door and damaged it. Marty had put in a claim and then fixed the door himself. More YAY! They had sent us the money from the insurance company. The next week another a letter came asking for ninety dollars as the hot water heater in the house had broken and they needed the money to fix it. The lesson to me was very clear. You will get what you need, but nothing extra!

We stayed five years in St. Thomas, from 1966 to October 1971. After we had been there for a while, I realized that in spite of its being a very lovely island with lovely climate and beautiful beaches it was a difficult post for me. So many different factors contributed to this understanding.

As it was small, roughly 13 miles long by 2 miles wide, its characteristics were more noticeable. I had always lived in big cities, with our focus being on family, work, friends and the immediate neighborhood. But in St. Thomas it was so small, one became aware of the situations prevailing in the whole island. The population was mainly in four different categories; native dark skinned St. Thomians, native white St. Thomians; Continentals, that is, those from the Continental United States: and native West Indians down-islanders who were working or staying there trying to get to the United States or just happy to be in U.S. territory, earning U.S. dollars and sending some home to their families. As it usually is, these groups mainly kept to themselves without much fraternizing.

The native white St. Thomians felt they had the edge and were clearly the bedrock of St. Thomas. They owned most of the businesses and still owned most of the land. Later when I had gone to work at H. Stern, an international jewelry store, I met a young woman from this population who also worked there. She and I became good friends, allowing me a peek into this society otherwise not obtainable by a "Continental". She told me a great story about her grandfather who loved to play cards. One night he got into a game; lost steadily and ended up selling St. John Island for $7.00 an acre to another player!

This level was not particularly interested in any new religion. The only one from this level of society that I know of was Knud Jensen who enrolled in 1961 in the Harmer home, becoming the first Bahá'í in the Virgin Islands. His father was of Danish origin, mother, St. Thomian. Knud was born in Denmark in 1917 and brought to the Virgin Islands as a baby. He was a strong, active Bahá'í, and died in St. Croix, Virgin Islands in 1987.

The native dark skinned St. Thomians were children born there, either from the 4th grouping of the down-islander West Indians or from the slaves brought here over the years by either the British, French, Spanish or the Danish all of whom ruled the islands at one time or another. The islands were finally sold to the United States in 1916 by Denmark. These offspring then thought of themselves as Americans, mingling with those from other islands. These were the ones that I found were more receptive to the Faith, and many became and stayed strong Bahá'ís. The first one in this grouping to become a Baha'i was Alma Lake in 1965. She lived in a project close to us and we visited with her often. While not an active teacher, she did attend the Bahá'í activities and events. She was a quiet, sweet woman.

St Thomas was also moving into the sea of materialism. It was U.S. territory and a free port. At any time of the year large cruise ships could be seen in the harbor. During Christmas time there would be as many as ten cruise ships docked there, all its travelers rushing into a concentrated area of shops downtown. The stores sold both cheap and expensive jewelry, liquor, tobacco, and lots and lots of cheaper souvenirs. These all were on the same block on the main street, which was approximately 200 yards long. The only other street in downtown, running parallel and was called "Back Street" but sold almost nothing to attract the tourists.

The earliest chance I had at teaching the Faith here happened one day when I went to lunch. It was at an open-air restaurant and I settled down to eat and read my book. Eventually I heard someone speaking to me. I looked up and at the next table a tall, good sized, good looking and very dark-complexioned man, with a big grin, saying 'Hi, can I buy a drink?' "No" I said, "I don't drink". "Oh, how about a beer then?" After that it became very clear, he was not going to leave me alone. I thought to myself, all right, if I can't read, you are going to hear about the Bahá'í Faith! We began to talk and an hour later it was also clear that this man, Ted Brown, was seriously interested in the Faith. I invited him to our home, making sure he understood I was married. He became a Bahá'í not too long after that. He also became a very good teacher of the Faith, bringing in several new Bahá'ís, all ladies!

As we settled in, we started having firesides in the style of the only ones we knew from California. As there was a great variety of peoples in St. Thomas, these turned out to be very successful. Also, Dorothy Behar was a great "attractor", she was one of those who act as a magnet for seekers and left the "teaching" to others. We had lots of young people attending our firesides, many of whom became Bahá'ís.

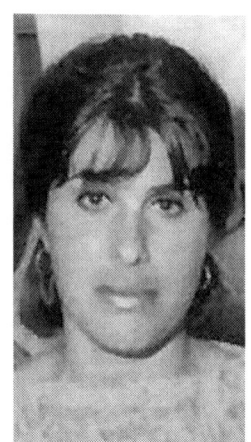

This as it developed, became a minor problem for me, as I was reported to the Local Spiritual Assembly as not teaching the Faith properly "...otherwise so many would not have become Bahá'ís so quickly".

I met with the Assembly and after a bit, was able to convince them that I did have enough knowledge necessary to teach the Faith to others.

In another encounter with a pioneer from the States, I once again ended up in front of the Assembly. She was "black" as the term went in the 1960's and another pioneer from the United States. I was so delighted to meet her! I was born and raised in Detroit, Michigan, which had a most deserved reputation as being one of the most racially prejudiced cities in the country. It had not been possible for me to have a "black" friend there so I was so happy to have a Bahá'í pioneer who could fill me in as to how her experiences had been growing up in the still divided atmosphere of the times. I began asking her question after question. She apparently misunderstood what I was doing and reported me to the Assembly as a racist. Oh my, that is not an easy thing to try to explain to others, especially when their decisions affect ones' whole life. Fortunately, I must have been able to make my motives understood to them, but unfortunately, she and I never became friends.

Frank, Judy and I made our first travel teaching trip in 1968. The following years, I made most of the following trips through the islands of the Caribbean taking our youngest daughter Judy with Lynn staying home with her father and grandmother. I eventually visited most of the islands over the years. My boss at H. Stern, Mrs. Hanna Steiner, who liked the Faith and me, would sigh when

ST. THOMAS | 19

First 19 Day Feast held on Montserrat, August 1968
2nd. L: travel teachers, Pat Paccassi, 1st. R: Frank Paccassi

I came to her at the beginning of summer, and say, "Ok, how long will you be gone this time?"

Travelling down island was a real education for me. I went to places where I had not even imagined existed and saw lifestyles totally unfamiliar to me. I learned new ways of describing things. An example of this was on one of the islands and looking at a large, beautiful tree. I asked one the local men what kind of a tree it was. He looked at for a time and said, "A shade tree".

The local Bahá'ís at that time were mostly not of influential people or those with a lot of financial means. On one trip to Nevis, we, Frank, Judy and I stayed at the home of the Claxton family who were the Bahá'í bedrock of the island.

It was a rather small house with many occupants. We were given the bedroom of the children. All three of us slept in the one bed. As it was summer, it was hot with very little breeze. In the daytime, the flies covered the bed and at night the mosquitoes replaced the flies. Judy was 10 and a restless sleeper. So combined with her tossing and turning in the little bed and the mosquitoes enjoying the "imported" blood, I did not fall asleep right away. Just as I had just fallen into a nice slumber state, I was awakened by a loud, loud cheery voice saying "Well, good morning everyone!" I was so startled that I sat straight up and said in a loud voice and definitely not with a non-Baha'i-like comment said, "What in the hell is that!" The sound immediately stopped. I later found out it was a radio show from St. Martin which came on every morning at 4.30 am. Nothing more was said about this by anyone. The next morning the radio didn't come until 7.00 am.

At the first meal we had there, I had expected that we would eat with the family, but instead were fed at a different time. The lady of the house put our food down and waited, watching us eat. Never did find out why for sure, but I later figured out that she was so unsure what she could feed us would be alright. So she had to stay and watch us and make sure we would eat what she had given us.

This family was very gracious, and we ended up having a wonderful time. It didn't take me long to figure out that I was really more comfortable with village people rather than the "upper level". I can do upper-level, but prefer villages.

Our firesides on the porch at night when all the neighbors came were great! I was born and raised in Detroit, Michigan which had a population of 3 million people. These new experiences in small village life as well as bugs in the dry foods, ants in the sweet things, flies and mosquitoes everywhere was perhaps made easier for me to be content here because when I was young my family had always gone camping all summer long. Life was also simple then; we slept in tents and my morning chore was to scoop the ants out of the food that they had managed to get into overnight.

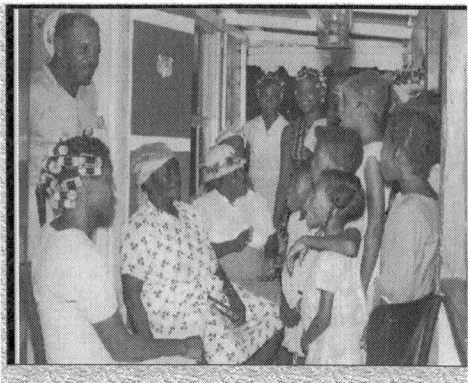
Meeting at Claxton home in Brown Hill, Nevis August 1968

I loved travel teaching. West Indians are a gracious people. They always give you the benefit of doubt, not simply judging that if you were white, you feel would you were superior and would act accordingly. They are generous, if they have two of something and you need one, they will share. The faults, of course, are there as well, but one learns what is appropriate during different situations.

My youngest daughter Judy, who usually traveled with me, was loved instantly. For years I was known as "Judy's mummy".

After we had been in St. Thomas for a year, the time for the formation of the first regional National Spiritual

Assembly of the Bahá'ís of the Leeward, Windward and Virgin Islands had come. It was April 1967. Hand of the Cause of God Dr. Ugo Giachery, representing the Universal House of Justice, and his wife, Angeline attended. At the time the National Spiritual Assembly was formed I was on the National Teaching Committee and as such was asked to give the report at Convention. I was really nervous, especially with a Hand of the Cause of God sitting next to me. But later when I looked at the photo of this taking place, I was truly cheered in that he did seem to be listening.

There were also many visitors from overseas. Many of them connected to Baha'i institutions who had worked for years helping the development of the Faith in the Caribbean Islands. Others were travel teachers who had made many teaching trips in the islands and felt that it was like the birth of a child. Altogether there were close to 100 attending. I was thrilled!

Those elected to this first Assembly were: Edwin Miller, from Grenada, Chairman, Jean Desert, from Guadeloupe, Vice-Chairman, Katherine Meyer, from St. Thomas, Corresponding Secretary, Henrietta Trutza, from St. Lucia, Recording Secretary, Ellerton Harmer St. Thomas, Treasurer, Thomas Hooper from St. Thomas, Lorraine Landau from Saba, Jeffery Lewis from Grenada, and Dorothy Schneider from St. Croix.

It is interesting to note that of the nine members of the National Spiritual Assembly of the Leeward, Windward and Virgin Islands, eight of the nine members were pioneers, all of whom were originally from the United States except Jean Desert who was from Haiti. Jeffery Lewis from Grenada was the only West Indian Bahá'í from within the National Spiritual Assembly jurisdiction.

22 | FROM ISLAND TO ISLAND

The following Bahá'í year, 125 BE or 1968-69, Katherine Meyer left the area to pioneer to a post in South America, creating a vacancy in the Assembly. In the by-election there were 13 votes for 13 single persons. As I had been traveling in the area for a few trips, my name was apparently the best known of the thirteen, and I was elected to the National Assembly.

L to R: Ellerton Harmer, Pat Paccassi, Wilfred Bart, Beverly Miller, Tom Millington, Lorana Kerfoot, Bill Nedden, Henrietta Trutza, and Edwin Miller.

The national area was later divided in 1972 into two national Bahá'í areas, the Leeward, and Virgin Islands and the Windward Islands.

In order to help with the consolidation of the new Bahá'ís we moved to Barbados after the mass teaching project in 1971. Both Frank and I were elected to the newly formed National Spiritual Assembly of the Bahá'ís of the Windward Islands.

The seat, Barbados, was later added to the official name, as Barbados did not consider themselves part of the Windward Islands. It then became the National Spiritual Assembly of the Bahá'ís of Barbados and the Windward Islands.

But in 1967 National Spiritual Assembly of the Leeward, Windward and Virgin Islands had a difficult task ahead of it. The islands included 4 languages, English, French, Spanish and Creole. It had 4 major currencies, the American Dollar, the French Franc, Barbados Dollar and Eastern Caribbean Dollar. These small islands were surrounded by large bodies of water, the Atlantic on one side and the Caribbean Sea on the other side. One good thing was that except for the French Islands, English was spoken everywhere else.

The French Islands are described as follows:

> FRENCH WEST INDIES*: The French overseas departments of Guadeloupe and Martinique in the Lesser Antilles, along with the island of St. Barthélemy and the French Portion of Saint Martin.

Within this grouping English was spoken on both St. Barthélemy and St. Martin. At first, however, the Assembly did not know that English was easily spoken on St. Barts. A desperate search was made for a travel teacher who spoke French. Roy Massey from the United States did make a trip to the island and was happy to report that English was widely spoken there. At a later date, Roy ended up as a pioneer residing in the French Islands.

The third year, the Assembly did not have a French speaking person on it. Thus in order to communicate with the French Islands a letter was written in English, sent to New York to be translated into French, then sent by mail to the proper French island, wait for an answer, then sent to New York to be put into English and sent back to St. Thomas. One could only hope that there was not an urgent matter to be dealt with. Later however, this was no longer a problem when the French speaking pioneers arrived.

Travel was also a challenge to be overcome as the members lived in islands from St. Thomas to the North and Grenada to the South. Air travel was very expensive. Some of the members who lived in the lower islands would often combine an Assembly meeting with stopping in islands to or from meetings to do teaching or conveying messages from the National Assembly.

It was also remarkable in that the first years the National Assembly was self-sustaining in its finances. Later however, it had to be subsidized by the

---

* American Heritage® Dictionary of the English Language, Fifth Edition.

Universal House of Justice.

There was a great need for pioneers in this newly formed national area. As a result, a flood, literally hundreds of prospective pioneers stopped in St. Thomas, the seat of the national headquarters to consult with the National Assembly before going to their post down island. This practice was not always as useful as one might imagine. For some, stopping in St. Thomas gave these prospective pioneers a look at and a taste of an entirely new lifestyle. It was easy living, lots of things to do, a relaxed atmosphere of people who came from the United States who kicked off their shoes, shirts and inhibitions in that order. Some Bahá'ís did not last long as pioneers. Many, however, did move directly to other islands where they served with devotion and dedication.

I have made a table showing the names, places and the dates of the pioneers and travel teachers up to 1984 when my research ends, this is a link to the information:

http://www.bahaihistorycaribbean.info/Complete_List_Pioneers_and_Travel_Teachers_to_LWVI_Web_View.pdf

Over the years one could almost predict which new pioneers would leave their posts soon. These were the ones who complained about almost everything, nothing suited them, and they invariably returned to their homeland.

Between 1959 and 1981, seven Hands of the Cause of God visited St. Thomas: Dr. Giachery, 1959 and 1967; Amatu'l-Bahá Rúhíyyih Khánum, 1970; Raḥmatu'lláh Muhájir, 1974; Jalál Khazeh, 1974; John Robarts, 1974; Paul Haney, 1977; and Enoch Olinga, 1977.

The visit of Rúhíyyih Khánum in June 1970 was a great honour and pleasure for our area. In looking back, it seems incredible that she was only there for three days! So much happened with activities for her, interviews with the media, courtesy calls on government officials, and meeting with the Bahá'ís.

I personally had the wonderful duty of driving her and her companion, Violette Nakhjavání during the visit.

At the airport saying goodbye, I watched Khánum go and felt as though I was losing my best friend. She turned around at that moment, saw my face, came back, and in a tone of voice mixed with annoyance and affection said, "Oh Pat" and gave me a kiss on the cheek.

Just before she and Violette arrived, I had received a call from one of our friends in Puerto Rico who asked if we could give hospitality to a team of young people. At that point, once the news had gone out that such a distinguished visitor was coming, all available hospitality was immediately filled. I apologized, but said it wasn't possible. After a brief hesitation, my friend asked if we had a back yard. I said "Yes", and he said "Great, I'll get together a tent and supplies and they can just stay in the back yard!"

It was now too late to back out. The team arrived just in time for the meeting. Eloy Enello, a young pioneer to the island was the coordinator. I took one look at the team consisting of several young, teenage boys and girls. This would not do, and promptly managed to get other places for the girls to stay, the boys stayed with me.

I had been assured that they would be self-sufficient and take care of everything themselves. That evening Eloy came into the house carrying a bag of rice and a sweet smile on his face. He hefted it in his hand and asked, "How much water should I use for this?" OK, I now had a team of lovely young Puerto Rican boys to care for! Evidently, what had been meant by self-sufficient was that the girls would take care of things like that. Eloy is second from the right.

The next night it rained, and I woke up the next morning, went downstairs, and saw wall to wall boys sleeping everywhere. I never regretted it as getting to know them and such a sweet young Eloy Enello was a privilege. He contributed so much in his Bahá'í life. In 1984, he founded Nur University in Santa Cruz, Bolivia. One can look him up in Wikipedia to see how extensive the contributions were made by him through this university.

During the teaching trip through South America that I made in 1985 with Meherangez Munsiff I met Eloy again. During our chat, he told me the following story.

"On one of the early visits of Dr. Muhájir I asked him what he saw for me in my future. He put his head back and after a bit said, "I see you travelling, travelling, and travelling".

Eloy then said to me, "And I haven't been off an airplane since!"

In 1965 a letter to the Local Spiritual Assembly of St. Thomas was received from the National Spiritual Assembly of the United States Property Goals Committee asking them to look for Ḥaẓíratu'l-Quds property costing between $10,000 to $12,000 U.S. dollars.

This, for some reason, did not become a priority until 1971, when the Local Spiritual Assembly of St. Thomas began to intensify its search for property sites. Here are before and after photos of the property that was eventually purchased in the downtown area of Charlotte Amalie.

In the early part of 1971, the National Assembly having been thrilled by the news of the Mass Teaching projects in the United States began to plan its own Mass Teaching project in the islands. This project was a true act of faith, as there was very little money in the National Fund to finance it. Nevertheless, a plan was adopted with me as coordinator. The original choice of Nevis for the project was not feasible as I could not find housing large enough to accommodate the team we anticipated. Barbados was chosen instead. This account of the project will be given during my Barbados recollections.

In 1971, a series of Oceanic Conferences was announced. The closest to St. Thomas was being held in Jamaica in May 1971. A cruise ship was chartered from the United States for the trip to the conference. It was designed to be a concerted program for the proclamation, expansion, and consolidation of the Cause.

Approximately 550 Bahá'ís from the United States sailed on this cruise ship called "The New Bahama Star". It sailed from Miami and stopped in St. Thomas and Puerto Rico picking up the Caribbean Bahá'ís on its way to the conference.

We had a great time on this ship. All the passengers were Bahá'ís. The ship accommodated them by closing the bars and the casino. Bahá'ís get on such a high when a large group gets together. One could almost feel sorry for the crew who were bombarded with firesides everywhere they turned. It also was a test for them in that the waiters relied on good tips from the people they served at their assigned tables. But, Bahá'ís do not sit in the same place all the time. They table hop and chat and visit and the poor crew could not count on one set of people at any time.

On the return trip the Bahá'ís in St. Thomas had arranged a simplified teaching plan during the several hour layover in St. Thomas. The first part had the Bahá'ís taking the short walk into town, rather than take taxies as was normal. This did arouse a lot of attention. However, the taxi drivers weren't too happy and in retrospect, a lot of others who watched the march probably just thought they were stupid or incredibly cheap, the noon day sun is very hot! But there were 172 enrollments that day!

Mass teaching had a lot of mixed emotions among the Bahá'ís. Most Bahá'ís were not neutral, they were either for it or against it. In St. Thomas there seemed to be more in the "against" than in the "for it" category. We all know what happens, or rather, doesn't happen when unified action is not taken.

The rest of our time in St. Thomas followed a pattern that seemed to hold over the years. One gets into a routine, teaching, assembly meetings, Bahá'í meetings and all the other activities that life brings us. It takes a lot of self-discipline to remember that you are where you are in order to promote the Faith, as well as maintaining the Bahá'í standard of living at all times. Everyone around you knows you are a Bahá'í and they watch closely to see if you practice what you preach. In the West Indies you are either "walking the walk" or "talking the talk".

After the 1971 mass teaching project held in Barbados, it was clear that the few pioneers on that island where not going to be able to handle the consolidation of all the new believers. Frank and I consulted, and we decided we would move to Barbados to help. After all it only seemed fair as I had coordinated the teaching project.

We then started a process which was to be our guide for the remainder of our pioneering. When the need arose, we answered the call and went. It wasn't always the same process in the beginning of each move, however. Some we initiated, others came about after Frank had lost a job and needed a new one. We would consult with the National Spiritual Assembly and they in turn would send us where the need was.

Our move to Trinidad was the only exception. This move was decided by our financial concerns. Frank had again lost his teaching job in St. Lucia in 1985 due to local people becoming available. We did not have savings that would sustain us and our social security from the United States would not kick in for another two years. He was now at retirement age in the Caribbean with no prospect of getting another job.

During a visit to Sacramento, California, I came in contact with Charyl and Keith Thorpe who had pioneered to Trinidad several years ago. They still owned a house there and Charyl said they would subsidize us. We could live in their house rent free. This subsidy would also include the rent money from the two apartments downstairs which we could use to maintain the property as well as for our own personal needs. Wow, talk about an offer one can't refuse!

It also turned out to be part of our overall plan from Bahá'u'lláh as it was here that I was to become part of the Institute Process which was just starting on the island. It's hard for me to find words to describe my feelings toward being introduced to this process. It was the next step in the development of the teaching in our area. We had tried so hard to consolidate after projects, but there was just never enough manpower or a consistent plan. This was an answer to the dilemma. I was asked to be on the Trinidad and Tobago National Bahá'í Institute Board of Directors and served as its secretary for the remainder of our time on the island. But more on time spent in Trinidad later.

In October 1971 we left St. Thomas and moved to Barbados. I had gone and ahead to find us a place to live in Belleplaine, Barbados. I remember leaving St. Thomas and walking towards the airplane and with each step I felt lighter, joyous, and free! It was a strange feeling, but I knew in spite of moving while we were not at all sure that we could stay on Barbados, it was the right thing to do.

| 4 |

BARBADOS:
OCTOBER 1971 TO MARCH 1976

The first time I spent a length of time in Barbados was in August 1970. I had planned a three-week teaching trip asking a few youth to join me. My daughters, Lynn and Judy, a young friend of ours, Michael Fanning, from Carmichael, California and a youth from St. Vincent, Don Providence, settled in a small village called Newbury. It was in the middle of the island and a delightful place to be. On the first night, after everyone had gone to bed, Michael called out in a strange, worried voice. We rushed into his room and he was pointing to the ceiling. We looked and the ceiling was covered with tiny blinking lights…fireflies…Michael had never seen them before.

We began the next day going around and inviting people to a meeting that night. In these early days, there were not the distractions one has today. No television, cell phones, and very few land line phones, you usually had to go to the police station to make a phone call. So that night we had a packed house! My favorite guest was an older lady who came to the meeting each night carrying her chair on her head. She wasn't going to have to stand like so many others.

We did end up enrolling many new youth in the Faith.

Near the end of project Frank was to make a visit to join us. Ethel Harris, a pioneer from St. Croix with whom I had been teaching here the year before was also joining us. As great luck would have it, Hand of the Cause of God, Enoch Olinga was also making a visit to Barbados. Frank and Ethel arranged their flight to travel with him from St. Thomas.

The flight was scheduled to have a short layover in Antigua. Frank knew that a young American pioneer family, Joyce and Jody Owen were serving the Faith there. Frank suggested a visit to them, and Mr. Olinga was delighted to do that. They reached the house, knocked on the door. Joyce answered and when she saw who her visitors were, she was first shocked and of course then delighted! A visit from a Hand of the Cause of God is a great honour.

Before they left Antigua, they had lunch at the airport. The young waitress served them, and Mr. Olinga said to her that he knew what tribe she was from in Africa. She drew herself up and said clearly "I am from Antigua."

After arriving in Barbados, Mr. Olinga was taken to the house of American pioneers, Karen and Phil Wood in the parish of Christ Church. I wanted so much to see him and invite him to talk at one of our meetings in Newbury.

When I arrived at the house he was resting, but hearing Karen and I chat, he came out to join us. He looked so tired that I hesitated to ask, but I did anyhow. He looked at me and asked me what it was like in Newbury. I thought a minute and said to him "Where you are staying now is like the city. Where I am staying is like the country." He broke into big smile, jumped up saying "Let's go!"

It was a wonderful meeting that night. Not only did all of

our neighbors come, but also Baháʼís from around the island. The meetings were all outside and he talked about the greatness of this time and how long it was destined to last.

After the meeting, the delighted Baháʼís gathered in our small house chatting for a long time. Mr. Olinga suddenly pointed at me and said, "I want you to move to Barbados." We were all startled and especially knowing how very hard it was for pioneers to stay in Barbados, we all laughed. Mr. Olinga raised his voice and said, "I have the power to make this happen." We all stopped laughing and I for one, was dumfounded. A note should be made here that one year later our family came to Barbados as pioneers and stayed five years. Frank eventually got a position teaching Science and Math in the public school system.

In the early part of 1971, a mass teaching project was planned by the National Spiritual Assembly to be an international endeavor. Having a very small amount of money in the National fund didn't seem to be pertinent. Nevis, a small island in the middle of the island chain was the first choice for the project. I was chosen to coordinate the project.

In 1971, an investigative trip to Nevis was made but no venue suitable for a project of this size was available. I then traveled to Barbados, to see if a site was available there. I first went to St. George Parish as it was in the middle of the island, and I had just last year held a small, successful teaching project in nearby Newbury. I also found a good-sized building with lots of built in bunks, a large dining room and a big kitchen. Perfect! It was currently empty as it was the housing provided for cane cutters during the season.

The Continental Board of Counsellors had been approached and asked to send someone to help us. They graciously sent an Auxiliary Board Member, Ruth Pringle. This woman turned out to be one of the most able, dedicated, devoted Baháʼís I was ever to have the privilege of knowing. She was a chatter, talking all the time and everything she said was interesting. Rúhíyyih Khánum called her "…a brilliant Baháʼí".

The National Assembly of the United States was also approached. They sent us a team of 3 Bahá'ís, Van Gilmer, Shirley Yarbrough and Jim Taylor. They were all experienced mass teachers having taught in several projects in the States. Van and Shirley were musicians as well. They were also welcome in that the majority of the overseas teachers preciously seen were white however these Bahá'ís had some colour to their skin.

Jim Taylor looked at our new housing, turned to the other members of the team and said, "Well, we've come full circle".

![Team with some friends in St. George's - 1971. Left to Right: Leroy Wharton, Ruth Pringle, Judy Paccassi, ---, Amanda Wrighton, Shirley Yarbrough, Van Gilmer, Pat Paccassi, Shirley Howard, Tony Harmer, Leon Sternberger, Errol Sealy, Don Providence, Diane Bourne, Mr. Lorde, Karen Wood]

Local Bahá'ís were also asked to participate in the project; Errol Sealy, Fitzgerald Callender, Diane Bourne and Leroy Wharton from Barbados, Don Providence and Shirley Howard from St. Vincent, Amanda Wrighton from St. Martin and Tony Harmer, a youth from St. Thomas. My daughter Judy, also a youth was part of the team as well.

Other teams arrived at later dates as a follow up. The New Era Trio, Charles and Sandi Bullock and Jeanne Rebstock from the United States, came in September to join the project after the first three weeks of the project were over and the original team left. Jim Taylor, Ruth Pringle and I stayed after the initial project. This group began to work on consolidation, but teaching also was involved, resulting in many more enrollments.

One of the new Bahá'ís, Burleigh Eastman, worked as a full-time teacher. He went out five days a week and never came back without enrollment cards. It was later found that it would have been better to send him out accompanied by an experienced teacher. Many of those who had been enrolled did not really understand what they were joining.

L to R: Phil Wood, Ruth Pringle, Karen Wood, Burleigh Eastman, Frank Paccassi, Pat Paccassi

This project was so much fun. All the members of the team grew to love each other and the people of Barbados. One could not have asked for a more unified group. And the teaching was so easy, people were very receptive to the Message of Bahá'u'lláh. In 3 weeks, we had enrolled 500 new believers. There is nothing more satisfying or exhilarating than teaching the Bahá'í Faith. And when those whom you are teaching also accept His Message, this is icing on the cake. Every day teams went out to reach new people and invite them to the nightly meetings.

The music was great. Shirley and Van singing together transformed everyone who heard them. One time we had arranged a radio broadcast for them. They started singing "Oh Bahá'u'lláh, oh Bahá'u'lláh" and just could not stop. The music and the words and the love that generated it were captivating. I can still hear the sweetness of those voices.

A lot of media exposure was available to us in those days. As I explained before without a lot of outside distractions, even media access was easily obtainable.

Many of the new Bahá'ís from the village began working with the team in the teaching work. This brought credibility to the Message brought to Barbados by "strangers". A hard core of local Bahá'ís developed and remained steadfast.

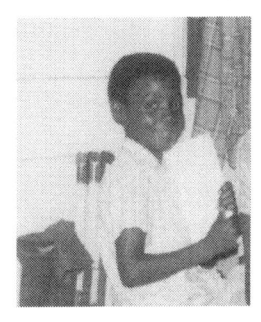

One of the favorite stories was about a young enrollee named David Watkins. He was 11 years old and on fire with the Faith. His first spiritual children were his grandparents. He also enrolled about 30 of his friends, a lot of whom were older than he was. What a sweet child he was, his love of Bahá'u'lláh was so strong that others could see, understand and embrace!

Another of our favorites was a blind man who was living in the village. He was in his house where Shirley Yarbrough was teaching another person near his window. He could hear them and later told us that he knew that everything she was saying was true and he wanted to join. He remained a steadfast and devoted Bahá'í.

The plan was to start teaching in our immediate area and then to move outward. At the end of the project in December all the 11 Parishes had new Bahá'ís.

Two Teaching Conferences were held. The first had 30 participants representing 1 Parish. The second had 67 participants representing 6 (of 11) Parishes. A cable was sent to the Universal House of Justice. In turn the Universal House of Justice sent a cable expressing their joy at the new believers who were arising to promote the Faith.

It was so unfortunate that the rest of our consolidation plan which was dependent upon the use of the schools as meeting places did not materialize. The Anglican Church at that time controlled all public schools. They of course were not happy with our teaching results and refused permission to use the public schools.

A bonus I received during the project was the news that on 21, August Hand of the Cause of God Dr. Varqá was on a plane that had a short layover in Barbados. I had found out however that he was unable to leave the plane. I immediately contacted the manager of the airport requesting permission to board the plane during the layover to talk to Dr. Varqá. Much to my surprise and delight, I received it, but with strict instructions that I and only I could board the plane. The whole team went out to the airport hoping to catch a glimpse of him.

The plane landed, passengers got off and I was told I could now go on board. I started out, looked back, seeing Ruth's face. It had such longing; I could not resist and beckoned her to join me. Dr. Varqá was in the doorway, waiting for us. Ruth and I stood there gazing up at his handsome face, with his shining eyes and soft voice. He talked to us until it was time for us to leave the plane.

We both floated back to the team. They immediately demanded to know what he had said. I looked at Ruth and she looked at me. It soon became clear that neither of us had really been listening, only gazing. The team was furious! They said, "You two talk all the time and now when you have something we really want to know, you don't talk." I can't say I blame them; I would have been furious too.

In December we planned to organize a teaching project in St. Vincent with a team of youth from Barbados. One seeming drawback however was a threatening volcanic eruption on the island. I was not in the least bit doubtful about going ahead with our plans. I did however end up having to visit each youth's parents with reassurances.

Here are the teams who were involved in the project:

L to R: myself as coordinator, Richard Miller, Myralene Moore, Monica Braithwaite, Leroy Wharton, Burleigh Eastman, Errol Sealy as trainee youth coordinator, and Lynn Paccassi.

Hendrick Branch and Don Providence from St. Vincent joined the team later in the project. Iris Guinals de Maul from Puerto Rico came to help as well.

We again picked a village in the central part of the island. There was a two-story building available for us. The upstairs was furnished as an apartment, but the downstairs was empty. We tried to get beds for the boys, but none were available. Some slept on cardboard, Errol Sealy slept on a crate of empty soda bottles, covered with cardboard. But never a word of complaint was heard.

Being youth, their boundless energy allowed them to work from early morning right through nightly meetings. The youth were able to attract and enroll many new youth in the Faith.

This project as all others do had its low points. The one in this project, in my estimation, was one rainy night when we decided to cancel the night meeting. At one point there was a prolonged knocking on the downstairs front door. I would not let the youth go and answer it. I thought it was some youth wanting to hang out with the team. The knocking persisted. I went downstairs to see who it was and inform them there was no meeting that night. Annoyed, I opened the door and standing there, very wet, and very, very annoyed, were some of the St. Vincent Bahá'ís who had come from town to join the team for the night meeting. Oops!

We also traveled to different villages during our stay there. One night in particular stands out in my mind. We went to Chateaubelair, one of the villages at the Northwest end of the island.

We hired a transport minibus to take us out and pick us up after the night meeting. The meeting itself was very successful, lots of interest and some enrollments. After the meeting we waited and waited for the transport to come for us. Finally, after deciding we would probably have to walk, the transport arrived.

The roads at that time were totally unlit, there was no moon that night and this was a winding road at best.

The driver met us on the road. As soon as we entered, it became obvious to all but one of the boys that the driver had too much to drink To make it worse he had brought his girlfriend with him, who was doing her best to get his full attention. Then in the back of the transport, the unaware boy, who was a talker at all times and being excited with the meeting, could not keep still. The rest of the team realized the drivers' condition and were very silent, praying I hoped, but not him. To make it worse, the driver was constantly turning around to hear what he was saying. I finally turned around to him and said in a low, serious voice, "If you don't stop talking, I am going to have the boys stuff your mouth with a sock!" Silence. Now we could all pray, and by the grace of God we got home safely.

The most outstanding occurrence, however, was the day when the team consulted about reaching our teaching goals. There had been a let-down, and nothing was really happening. I wanted to come up with something that would inspire and encourage. I told them if we make our teaching goals, we will send a cable to the Universal House of Justice. These were for the most part new Bahá'ís, but they were inspired and energized. A few days later when the goals had been reached, the whole proud team went into town and sent a cable to the Universal House of Justice.

A few days later we received an answering cable:

> "Overjoyed outstanding success Saint Vincent Mass Teaching Express our warm commendations West Indian Team Their praise-worthy efforts STOP Urge immediate follow up deepen new believers begin process development prospective new community STOP Assure prayers Shrines your devoted labours expand Faith."

The rest of the project went smoothly! The team went home to Barbados, happy and satisfied with their teaching efforts on St. Vincent.

After the mass teaching project had ended in Barbados in December 1971 it became obvious that with the 2200 enrollments over a 6-month period, more help was needed to work with the consolidation plan. It was a plan that had been devised by Ruth Pringle. When I was on Pilgrimage in 1972, Ian Semple, a member of the Universal House of Justice, commented on it at a meeting with the Bahá'ís stating that it was one of the best he had ever seen.

Frank and I consulted, and we decided to move to Barbados to help with the consolidation. He quit his job, he and Lynn packed up the house, and I went ahead to find us a place to live.

The family, Frank, Pat, Lynn, Judy and Grandma Snyder arrived in Barbados in October 1971. For this move we had to leave our registered French Poodle, Robbie, behind with a family who was happy to get him. Barbados law at that time required that all pets brought into the island be sent to England for a six months quarantine period.

I had found a nice house in the parish of St. Andrew. It was on the opposite side of the island's capital. I'm not sure if my decisions to live as far away from capital cities was by conscious thought or not, but in the majority of moves, that is exactly what I looked for in all of our moves as well.

Our landlady, Mrs. Rock, owned many businesses on the island, including prefabricated houses. The yard where they put them together was next door to our house. In looking back, I find it hard to believe we lived there for five years with no trace of annoyance from us at the noise that business had to have generated.

Mrs. Rock was a really nice lady. When we had to leave Barbados going to St. Vincent for a short period after having used up our visa extensions to stay, she let us leave all of our belongings in the house and didn't charge us rent while we were gone. All of us felt sure we would eventually be able to stay in Barbados. Another time, I had gone to pay our rent, and she began to talk about how high prices for everything had gone up. I began thinking "And so is our rent about to go up". But she concludes by saying "So I have decided to lower your rent". Never before, nor since, has that happened to me or to anyone I know!

Frank began looking for a job in Barbados. The first place he applied was a company listed as H.A.R.P., meaning High Altitude Research Project. This would seem to be a job for which he was highly qualified, having worked in the space industry in California. He went several times to talk to them but was never offered a job. Years later we were told that they had heard it was a United States CIA operation. If so, no wonder they hadn't hired him.

He then began to apply for a teaching position in Science and Math, as he had a degree in Physics. But there was not much luck there as well. We did have some savings from St. Thomas and lived on that until it was gone. Then Foreign Goals subsidized us until Frank got a job teaching in the school system. It was a lot cheaper to live on Barbados at that time with an exchange of $1.98 BDS to one United States dollar. For example, our weekly food bill was $35.00 BDS dollars a week.

During the 1971 mass teaching project, Ruth Pringle started to encourage me to go on Pilgrimage. That had never entered my mind and besides Frank was not working. After my first resistance I decided that it was a great idea and applied. Much to my surprise I was given a date right away to come in February 1972. Frank still didn't have a job.

Then, Hand of the Cause of God, Dr. Muhájir made one of his lightning trips to the island in January 1972. Because he was in and out of islands so quickly, I asked him if he knew what the friends called him. He said "No" I replied, "The lightning Hand" He laughed and said, "Do you know what they call me in India?" I said "No", and he said, "The missing Hand."

When he heard that I was going on Pilgrimage, he immediately began to encourage me to make a travel teaching trip around the world at the same time! Wow.

As much as I disagreed, he persisted and as he was leaving the island, and we were in the airport having a cup of coffee, he began to outline where I should go, how long to stay and what to do in each place. He told me where I should teach and where I should learn. He also said "...and you must be back for your National Convention."

L to R: Pat, Karen, Dr. Muhájir

Karen Wood another pioneer was also there, and as he began to give his outline, she began scribbling furiously on a napkin. It was the only piece of paper she could find.

I went into a semi-state of shock. It was simply too much to process and certainly way too much to expect to materialize. But that did not stop Karen and I from taking it to our travel agent, Mr. Ince. I told him that I had to be back by the middle of April. He looked at it and said "Oh Mrs. Paccassi, a trip like this could not be possible. You are traveling to fourteen countries. The schedules just won't work." Karen and I stayed with him and he reluctantly agreed to try.

Several days later, he called and told us "It was amazing. I tried and tried to book the flights from Barbados and home again. But it wouldn't work, so for some reason, I decided to try it backwards, and all the flights fell into place!"

Wonderful, but Frank still doesn't have a job, and savings just about gone.

At this point, I had to begin to send my passport to countries where I would need a visa to enter. The last country I needed had an embassy in the United States. Off it went.

During my wait for all this to materialize, Bahá'í life went on as usual. One of the things that happened was a teaching trip to another island. However, the tricky part was going to be how to get back into Barbados without my passport.

In those days, travel was much easier and more relaxed. People who were waiting for disembarking passengers could go outside on a second story balcony to wait and watch for them. I got off the airplane, slowly making my way to immigration, organizing my story as to how I didn't have a passport. I heard a voice calling my name, looked up at the balcony. There was Frank and Bill Nedden waving to me. I went over and Frank waves my passport in the air and drops it straight into my hands. Hurrah, another problem solved. But Frank still didn't have a job.

I am always amazed and surprised the way things work out when one relies on God. Dr. Muhájir arrives in January, rearranges my Pilgrimage itinerary to now go around the world and my flights are booked. Frank still does not have a job. A few weeks before I am to leave, a check arrives in the mail. It was from St. Thomas and reflected a check for retroactive salary payment of the time when Frank worked in the US Virgin Islands. It was exactly the amount I needed to go on my trip, with a little bit left over! I started on my trip, happy and full of joy. What a remarkable man Frank was! He had no problem with my going on Pilgrimage using funds sent to him.

I had been told by Dr. Muhájir that I should be back in Barbados by April 1972, the date of the formation of the first National Spiritual Assembly of the Bahá'ís of the Windward Islands.

The stories from this trip around the world have been put on a DVD by Joyce Olinga in 2013. It is called "Pat Paccassi's Incredible 1972 Global Travel Teaching Trip". It is available at Olinga Productions, PO Box 1423, Maryland HTS Mo or OlingaProductions@mac.com.

The last stop of my global trip was to the Bahá'í National Headquarters in Wilmette, USA, I met with Eileen Norman, secretary of the Foreign Goals Committee. I had great news for her in that I had found a job for Frank in Japan. Some pioneers owned an English-speaking academy and were happy to have him as one of their teachers. I had looked in all the places I went, but this was the first solid lead and I loved everything about the country.

Eileen said that probably would not happen, as they had received a cable from the Universal House of Justice saying that we were to stay in Barbados. We were to be subsidized if necessary. I went into a real tizzy. This was news that was not easily assimilated! How they even knew about our not being able to find a job in Barbados was mysterious to me. My whole system collapsed, and I caught the worst cold I had ever had in my life. But that sure settled our dilemma and stay in Barbados we did.

I did find out later that the Universal House of Justice had become aware of our predicament via the Foreign Goals Committee seeing it mentioned in the minutes of the National Spiritual Assembly of the Windward Islands, and again picked up by the World Centre seeing their minutes. This is quite a Bahá'í grapevine we have!

I arrived home in Barbados just before the Convention. It was a wonderful convention held at the University of the West Indies.

Nineteen delegates from our islands, Barbados, St. Vincent, Grenada and St. Lucia were present. Rúhíyyih Khánum was the representative of the Universal House of Justice. Her cousin, Jan Bolles Chute accompanied her. They stayed 10 days and had extensive coverage from the media.

We also had the bounty of having Rúhíyyih Khánum and Jan Chute for dinner one night as well as Edson Branch and Don Providence from St. Vincent.

44 | FROM ISLAND TO ISLAND

Seated L to R: Rúhíyyih Khánum, Grandma Snyder, Jan Chute

Standing L to R: Pat Paccassi, Edson Branch, Lynn Paccassi, Don Providence, Frank Paccassi

As we were finishing dinner, I asked Khánum if she would like another piece of Lasagna. She said yes, reached for it, paused and asked if we were having dessert. I replied "Yes", and she asked, "What is it?" I told her Lemon Meringue Pie. She sat back, telling me she would wait. Khánum also showed me how to put on the Sari I had bought in India. Forgive me, but these personal memories are so precious to me I feel I must share, and it shows the very human side of great Bahá'ís not always seen.

At dinner that night Khánum asked about how it was progressing with our efforts to stay on Barbados. But as there was little to tell, she specifically asked me to let her know. But when we finally got the news that Frank had gotten a teaching job here, I couldn't make myself write her with this news. She had so much to do and so little free time, I felt really uneasy taking up her time with our news.

The next year we attended the International Convention in Haifa. The photo is L To R: Iris Guinals de Maul, Frank, ____, and me in Haifa.

I was walking in one of the large meeting rooms and across the room I could see Khánum. She looks up, spots me and in a clear, loud voice, says to me "You were supposed to let me know what happened". Oops, I was embarrassed, stammered something and got out of her sight. The next morning, she, in her opening address to the Convention, began going on about the need for good communication needed by the Bahá'ís. Oops, now I've gotten a whole room of Bahá'ís at International Convention hollered at as well me.

At the national convention in Barbados the first baby naming ceremony was held for Violette Suzette Marjorie whose parents were George and Norma Howard from St. Vincent. Rúhíyyih Khánum was the witness to this ceremony.

Just before the voting for the new National Spiritual Assembly was to start, one of the delegates, in a long, roundabout way, hoping to sound delicate, began to ask if someone could vote for someone who was not really yet settled and was living on another island rather than where one's belongings were, etc. Rúhíyyih Khánum finally broke in and in that tone of voice only she could muster, said "Of course you can vote for the Paccassis".

Those elected to the first National Spiritual Assembly of the Bahá'ís of the Windward Islands were:

Seated: L to R: Phil Wood, Chairman, a pioneer from the United States; Frank Farnum, Vice Chairman from Barbados; Rúhíyyih Khánum; George Howard from St. Vincent; and Frank Paccassi, Treasurer a pioneer from the United States.

Standing: Karen Wood, Secretary a pioneer from the United States; Auxiliary Board Member Marjorie Harmer, a pioneer from the United States; Hazel Beckles, from Barbados; Carol Haynes, a pioneer from United Kingdom; Diane Bourne, from Barbados; Pat Paccassi, Recording Secretary, a pioneer from the United States.

In October 1972, the official name of the National Assembly had to be changed from the "National Spiritual Assembly of the Bahá'ís of the Windward Islands" to the "National Spiritual Assembly of the Bahá'ís of Barbados and the Windward Islands" as Barbados considered itself as a separate island not as a part of the Windward Islands. The National Assembly was also incorporated at the same time.

This was a very active National Assembly. It planned all different kinds of events to deepen, consolidate and encourage new teaching. One of these events was a Teacher Training Institute held in Barbados in December 1973. The venue was a large rented house in Martin's Bay.

Twelve students from three islands attended at the invitation of the National Assembly. The tutors were a distinguished and experienced group. A Counsellor, Rowland Estall, his wife Vivian Estall from Antigua, Auxiliary Board Members, Shirley Mather from the U.S. Virgin Islands, and Hopeton Fitz-Henley from Jamaica, and well-known international travel teacher and pioneer, Shamsi Sedeghat from Trinidad and Tobago. Shirley Yarbrough a pioneer to Barbados and I were the coordinators.

It was a great institute, everyone learned and most of the students became good teachers of the Faith in their home islands. After the event was over, however, we were told that one of girls had become pregnant. Oh my! At all the following training institutes there was a lot more emphasis on chastity and purity.

After the Mass Teaching Project in 1971, Shirley Yarbrough returned a year later as a pioneer. It was a great blessing for Barbados. Most of the pioneers who had come before her had been white. Not only was she dark skinned in this dark skinned island, she had a wonderful, cheerful personality and a great singing voice. Everyone who met her immediately joined her vast fan club. She was able to obtain a teaching position as a music teacher, a job she kept until she retired. She later married Carl Ishmael, a Barbadian. She was also appointed in 1974 as the first Auxiliary Board Member for the Windward Islands by Counsellor Rowland Estall. Her first appointment of an assistant was Errol Sealy, who later in life was appointed the first West Indian Counsellor for the Windward Islands area. As of this date, November 2018 she still resides in Barbados. Her husband, Carl, however, died a few years ago.

I should state here that I did not mean in any way to belittle the pioneers who were white. Indeed, I have always thought it was a great way to demonstrate that not all white people are prejudiced. Bahá'ís truly believe in the beauty of the oneness of mankind.

As this Nation Spiritual Assembly was elected in 1972 the members became eligible to participate in the election of the Universal House of Justice in 1973. We all wanted to go and cast our votes in Haifa, Israel!

It was in this time frame that our family continued to receive help in such unusual ways that it could only be part of God's bounty.

Frank and I were both delegates that year and we only had enough money for one air fare and expenses. I had been on Pilgrimage and taken a teaching trip around the world the preceding year. It was clearly Frank's turn.

When we had travelled from St. Thomas to Barbados, we had shipped all of our goods air freight. Everything had arrived safely except two boxes. Eventually we received a call from Eastern Airlines telling us that our boxes had been found. We went to the Cargo hanger; they took us outside and there sat our two boxes. They had been there the whole time, out in the weather. We opened the boxes knowing that whatever had been in the boxes had to be ruined as there had been a lot of rain recently.

In one box there were old clothes and miscellaneous goods. In the other box, however, was Frank's collection of early Marvel comic books. They were water soaked and had lost most of their collectors value. Frank put in a sizeable claim based on catalogue prices, but as the insurance claim did not arrive by return mail it faded from our memories. Yes, you probably guessed it. That is just what happened. The cheque arrived in time for both of us to be able to travel to the International Convention. I now regretted that I had earlier made such a fuss about Frank dragging around with us this large bunch of comic books!

Other pioneers arrived over the next few years. In 1973, Laurie Fanning, arrived from Grenada where she had been pioneering with her parents Pat and Chuck Fanning in Grenada. Laurie returned to the states to further her education and returned in 1976 staying until late in 1994. She also added much to the community, her music abilities and her marriage in 1977 to a local Barbadian, Errol Sealy, having made a statement that Bahá'ís lived as though mankind was one, not just preach it.

In 1974, Roy and Cynthia Carlton, from the United States, also an interracial married couple arrived and served in Barbados until Roy died in 1981. Cynthia stayed a few years longer. They first lived in St. Lucy, a goal parish and later served as caretakers at the National Bahá'í Centre. Cynthia would say about their teaching efforts in their parish far from the capital, "Every day we would sally forth to do battle".

In 1975, Emily Kramer, from the United States, arrived to serve here until 1978. She then moved to St. Lucia which was a goal island and lived in the village of Laborie. Emily had originally come as a Peace Corps volunteer but spent time with Bahá'í work as well. She served on the National Spiritual Assembly and attended the International Convention in Haifa in 1978.

A sad-funny story with Emily happened when she was living in St. Lucia. She lived on a restricted budget and drove a car that reflected that especially when looking at the four smooth tires on her car. At one point during her stay a relative had died and left her a sum of money. The first thing she did was to buy a whole set of new tires. YAY, no more stopping all the time to get a tire patched. She went to bed that night in Laborie, woke up the next morning and went out to go to town. OH MY! During the night someone had stolen all four of her new tires replacing them with tires just as smooth as the ones she had just replaced.

After we left in 1975, Nell Gibson and Karen Lindley pioneered in 1978, from the United States. They settled in the St. Andrew Parish and lived in the same house in Belleplaine in which we had lived and loved for five years. I later saw Karen in the States and had an interview with her about their time in Barbados. At some point I hope to have all the interviews I took available for all to read. However, at this point, they are only on my tapes, DVD's and computer, plus copies which were sent to the Bahá'í World Centre Archives Department.

We had settled ourselves in Belleplaine, but Frank still did not have a job. He looked everywhere including schools, but nothing materialized. The extension visas we needed from the government to stay on the island were getting harder and harder to get. Finally, in May 1972 we were told we had to leave the island. Oh my, but remember we had been told to stay on Barbados by the Universal House of Justice. No contest there, but now, how to proceed. We decided to go to the nearby island of St. Vincent.

When we got there, Mr. Edson Branch a local Bahá'í and good friend had arranged a place for us to rent. We moved in, and it wasn't more than a few days when our landlord came to us and told us we had to move out! What! Why? He told us that when he agreed to have us in his house, he didn't know we were Bahá'ís. Mr. Branch then graciously asked us to stay with him.

We stayed with him for a bit, but eventually rented our own house. It was a lovely house, overlooking the sea, but it was up a high hill, not uncommon in St. Vincent. We didn't have a car, so we all developed great leg muscles.

However, it was in this house that two major things occurred. One, Grandma fell and broke her hip. While she was very brave and strong, eventually after we moved back to Barbados, she ended up staying in bed. Always cheerful, never complained but was now bed-ridden.

The other thing was connected to the girls' education. When we moved from a United States territory to Barbados, a British based territory, the two education systems were not compatible.

While we were staying in St. Vincent, a young travel teacher, Marta Kelsey, about Lynn's age came on a teaching trip. She was from a well-known and respected Bahá'í family in the States. She and Lynn got along very well. After much back and forth, it was decided that Lynn would go back to the states with her, live with their family and finish high school. It was not easy to let her go, but it was what was best for her at the time. After all, she could return to us at a later date.

As for Judy's education, I ended up home schooling her after we returned here from St. Vincent in September 1972.

It was during one of my trips to and from St. Vincent to Barbados for National Assembly meetings that I almost was denied entry into Barbados. In line at immigration I was before an older man, all decked up in a white uniform complete with medals and tassels, quite unlike the ordinary immigration officer.

I showed him my passport which, due to my recent trip around the world contained lots of pages and entries. He scanned this carefully and asked in a belligerent tone of voice "Just where do you live?" Oh boy, if he refuses me entry into Barbados, I am in big trouble. So, I think a minute, waiting for an idea, then pull myself up to my full 5'1", and in the iciest, ugliest American tone of voice I can muster say "My permanent address is in St. Thomas, and I have a home in St. Vincent and Barbados!"

Now his face begins to change, you could almost hear him thinking, "Oh, oh, who is this lady?", and then his face changes more and it looks like he's now thinking, "Oh, oh, I could end up walking a beat in a remote part of Barbados again". So he then puts on a big smile and with a vigorous slam, stamps my passport and says, "Have a nice visit".

When we left Barbados for St. Vincent, we left Karen Woods phone number as a contact with the schools where Frank had applied. One day, while in St. Vincent, a call came from Karen that she had just gotten a call and Frank was being offered a teaching position! YAY. Even though he had never taught school before, only working as an engineer they evidently felt his BS in Physics qualified him to teach Science and Math.

It was helpful to us as well as at that time there were not enough local people with advanced educational degrees. At one of the schools where he taught, only he and the headmaster had a university degree. Another factor on Barbados was that those who did have degrees would not accept a job if it was not in their field. On other islands however we found that if a local person could not find a job right away, they would take a teaching position until one opened up in their field, but not on Barbados.

We happily returned and continued our five year stay on Barbados.

As there had eventually been 1500 enrollments from the recent project on the island and no places available to hold meetings, and very few Bahá'ís who were working in the process, the consolidation of the new Bahá'ís became daunting. We did the best we could and all of us spent as much time as possible going into communities and looking for the new Bahá'ís.

Some of the time it was easy finding those who welcomed us, and we would spend part of the time chatting, getting to know one another, and some time in deepening.

However, it was not always easy and once in a while even funny. Frank had an experience that over the years he and I would recall and still laugh about. Frank walked up to a small house in one of the villages, asking for one of the men whose name was on an enrollment card from the project. He waited and in due time a child who had answered the door came back pointing to the field behind the house saying "There he goes" and sure enough there he was, racing across the field pulling on a pair of pants as he went!

Another of my favorite responses was when a child again finally answered the door and we asked to talk to her Mommy, she said "My Mommy says she's not home".

But I think the most interesting and intriguing attempt at locating Bahá'ís on that long list happened to Frank Fernandes. It was many years after we left

Barbados. The National Spiritual Assembly had begun to make another attempt to reach the people on the list. Frank had always been an active teacher of the Faith. He was sent to a poorer part of the capital area to start there.

He relates that as he moved from house to house, he became aware of a sound that had no origin he could see. It sounded like horses walking. He then noticed that when the noise stopped and he knocked at a door, it was a house where one of the people lived. During this process, one time when he knocked at the doors near where the sound had stopped, he did not find any more of those on the list. He looked around and saw a path leading in another direction. He started up the path and the sound started up again. Here he found a few more people.

He walked a bit further and ahead saw a little-old-lady and stopped to talk to her. All of a sudden, the lady looked up over his shoulder, her eyes got wide and her mouth dropped open and she saw through the "veil" those who were accompanying Frank. He looked around and he too saw the horses and riders that were with him that day!

The phrase that I thought of when I heard this story, which I didn't doubt for a moment, was "Mount your steeds, O heroes of God". (God Passes By, Pages 35-48, US Bahá'í Publishing Trust, 1979 second printing; Pages: 412)

Our experience in the earlier days was that a lot of the new Bahá'ís were not interested any more as we did not have a place where we could meet. Everyone asked, "Where is your church?" Their experience in religion had not included going to someone's home to worship, not being expected to transform one's own character, nor to become involved with the process of helping others as well. A minister or priest did that.

A funny incident happened during an early visit of Counsellor Artemus Lamb. He was traveling with one of the friends in the eastern part of the island away from the capital. A car passed them, and he exclaimed "That man looks just like John Robarts!" Now Mr. Robarts was a Hand of the Cause of God, and most certainly would not be expected to be seen riding in a car in a remote part of our island where no one, especially a Counsellor, would not know he was there! So the incident was forgotten.

It wasn't too long after that Mr. Robarts contacted the Bahá'ís and said he was on the island and would be happy to meet the friends and the National Assembly.

Meeting with the National Spiritual Assembly:

R to L: Pat Paccassi, Errol Sealy, Shirley Yarbrough, Phil Woods, Carol Haynes, Ida McCray, Frank Paccassi, Hand of the Cause of God, John Robarts, Frank Farnum, Mozart Newton

The next chapter in the story has Mr. Robarts' telling us the story of his being in the other side of the island and seeing a man riding in a car which passed him and his wife, Audrey, on the road. Mr. Robarts said he had said to her "That man looked just like Artemus Lamb!"

Mr. Robarts family history in Barbados is very interesting. His grandfather was born on the island. While I am not sure of the time frame, Mr. Robarts said that he had been told that there was a big hurricane set to hit the island. His grandfather's mother was in her late stages of pregnancy and was very afraid. She went to a large outdoor oven that was used for baking bread and climbed inside. During the storm, the child was born. Mother and child were unharmed, and they named the baby Tempest.

One of the ways of community building that was tried was to hold a social outing called an Excursion. These were normally held by various groups at the beach and were always well attended.

In the summer of 1973, the National Spiritual Assembly decided to hold a Bahá'í Excursion. Notices went out via the local and only radio station called Rediffusion which was wired into all Barbadian houses.

Our notice said that a bus would pass the villages and the Bahá'ís were invited to attend the event. Errol Sealy was asked to accompany the bus making sure that every village with Bahá'ís was visited. At the appointed day, Errol set out on the bus and went around the island. He finally arrived at the beach site and he was the only one on the bus! None of the Bahá'ís had decided to come, not even for an excursion. Oh my, had it happened to anyone other than Errol, I am not at all sure they would have survived it! That was a serious, embarrassing test but Errol only got stronger as his future appointment as a Counsellor proved.

And if that wasn't enough for that day, a few of the Bahá'í boys showed up drinking. Well, it was an Excursion wasn't it, not a Bahá'í meeting.

One of our fellow Bahá'ís in Belleplaine, the village we had settled in was a gentleman named Reginald Barrow. He was an older man, very distinguished and well known in Barbados. For one thing he had been an Anglican Minister and was called by his religious title "Bishop" by all but the Bahá'ís for as long as I knew him. His son was also the current Prime Minister of Barbados.

He was a lovely man, kind, gentle, soft spoken, with something nice to say about everyone. He had become a Bahá'í in the United States. He was the preacher of a congregation in the Southern part of the country. When he heard of the Faith he joined immediately and brought all of his church members with him.

Reggie and Frank having a good chat.

There is correspondence between him and the U.S. National where he indicates a desire to pioneer for the Faith. He did end up doing that and was in St. Vincent first, then eventually to Barbados.

As his former occupation as a preacher was no longer possible for him, he ended up teaching in a public school. He was also instrumental in helping Shirley Yarbrough get a position teaching music in the school system as well. Just before we left Barbados, Frank was looking for a position in the same school where he and Shirley taught. If this job did not materialize, we would have to leave the island, which we did not want to do. Frank and I were saying prayers one day when we knew that possibility was being considered. During the prayers, Frank stopped, looked up and said, "I'm not getting the job". Sure enough, he didn't. But more on that comes later in this story.

Grandma Snyder went into Cardiac Failure in 1975 at the age of 90. Her doctor said she had about three months to live. I quietly had a carpenter start to make a casket from Green Heart, one of the hardest woods we had on the island and well fitted the description of what Bahá'ís should be buried in as stated in the Kitáb-i-Aqdas, the Bahá'í Most Holy Book.

I also came to the realization that I had not even considered where we were going to bury her. Oh my. The only cemetery in Belleplaine belonged to and was behind the Parish Church. We did not exactly have any friendly associations with the Minister.

I then thought of our friend, Reggie. We called him and asked his advice as to what we could do. He immediately volunteered to talk to the Minister and came back with the good news that she could be buried in their cemetery. I never did ask nor wanted to know what he had said, but I was sure happy with the results. We buried her the same day she died with the service in the Church. It was a lovely service, and everyone was happy with it.

She was the first pioneer to die at her post in the Windward Islands. Not too shabby! Her tombstone has a nine-pointed star, a quote from the prayer "Refresh and Gladden my Spirit" and identifies her as a Bahá'í Pioneer.

I still always ask the Bahá'ís to go to her gravesite when they can and say some prayers for her. As I remember, her only hesitation in coming pioneering with us was that no one would ever visit her grave. I do imagine that where she is buried, many more visit her than if she had been buried in California.

I miss my Grandma; she was a lovely lady. All the time she lived with us, I can never remember her complaining about anything. That in itself to me is amazing. She also used to say the Table of Ahmad for me whenever I was on a teaching trip. So much of what I do or have done I am sure is the result of others who prayed for me. And I am very grateful!

Other recollections about Grandma include her "chatting" abilities. She loved to chat! Everywhere she went, as the saying goes, she never met a stranger. In the store, on the street, in an airplane and especially in local corner shops, she would "chat them up" as the saying goes here. We would be in an area where I had never lived before, nor had she, but the first time I visited any local shop, everyone knew my whole story…oh, it was a good thing she liked me!

She was in good health right up to the end. The only drawback in the last years was the broken hip where she ended up bedridden, but there wasn't any pain connected to that.

Another reason was that she would now have a proper Bahá'í funeral. For several years she had insisted that she was to be cremated when she died. It seems somewhere in her past a Methodist minister had told her to do this otherwise he said, the world would soon be filled up with nothing but cemeteries.

Nancy Cole-August, a pioneer to St. Lucia and a wonderful talented artist did an oil painting of me and Grandma. It hangs right where I can see it easily, and I always smile when I look at it.

Grandma and I had many discussions about her being cremated with neither of us changing our opinion. Some minister had told her that if everyone kept being buried, there soon would be no space left on Earth! When we moved to St. Thomas and whenever I went on trips, and visitors came she would talk to them about it as well. It seems one of the visitors suggested that she write the Universal House of Justice and ask them. WOW, OK…that would not have occurred to me.

But that is exactly what she did, and received a wonderful, loving overall explanation of what should be done and why. She immediately changed her position and was now ok with being buried. This letter was later published in the book "Lights of Guidance" compiled by Helen Hornby. It is letter # 669, Page 201.

Helen and her husband Charles Hornby had pioneered to Ecuador. I stayed with them when I was traveling as a companion to Meherangez Munsiff (in the photo) on her teaching trip to all the countries throughout South America in 1985. It was a great opportunity for me and a great trip; lots of fun, lot of laughter, met so many new wonderful people, saw Eloy Enello, and didn't even have to do the work, that was all Mrs. Munsiff's department.

Back to Grandma, when I think of this process that Grandma went through, I am awed. Here she is having become a Bahá'í on her 80th birthday, now serving as a pioneer in St. Thomas. Writes a letter to the Universal House of Justice asking about something she has steadfastly believed in for a long time. When the answer arrives, contrary to this belief, she immediately adjusts her thinking. Imagine learning the lesson of obedience when you are in your 80's!

I was so relieved; I had not been able to reconcile myself to having my beloved Bahá'í grandma cremated contrary to Bahá'í law. But had she written a will I would have not had any choice. God is good!

However, there are others who were not so fortunate. When Reggie Barrow who had helped us so much with Grandma's burial passed away, he was buried by his son as an Anglican, even though Reggie had written a will specially stating that he wanted to have a Bahá'í funeral and burial. Shirley Yarbrough did go to the son, who was still the Prime Minister asking that Reggie's wishes be carried out, but to no avail.

It was in either late 1975 or early 1976 when Frank gave one of the biggest surprises that he had ever done either before or since. I was at home eating my lunch and reading my book in my bed, as I did usually. I heard his voice in the kitchen and was sorta surprised to hear him, though he did teach classes at the school that was directly behind us.

I looked up, he came charging into the bedroom and behind him was this lovely young woman. I blinked and he starts talking right away, saying she wants to hear more about the Faith. What, who is this and why would you bring someone into our bedroom anyhow, never mind to hear about the Faith?

It turned out that she was Yvette Clarke, one of the teachers at his school. They got chatting, and as one could expect, he began to tell her about the Bahá'í Faith. She was indeed interested and became a Bahá'í not too long after that. We did put her in touch with Shirley Yarbrough who also was very instrumental in teaching her the Faith.

Yvette soon began to serve the Faith in ever advancing ways. She was quickly appointed as an Assistant to the Auxiliary Board Member; next she was elected to the National Spiritual Assembly and then was appointed as an Auxiliary Board Member. All of this took place in less than a year. She was so capable and had such potential it was all laid upon her one right after another.

As I feared, there was too much pressure on her as a brand new Bahá'í. She also was engaged to a young man who was not a Bahá'í and not particularly open to it. She did try and went on teaching trips, etc. But it did become too much for her to handle and she was not seen around after that. I have always felt really bad about that and wished it had all been handled more wisely.

The National Spiritual Assembly began to look for Temple property in 1975 and by January 1976 10 acres of land had been found and purchased. It was located in the Parish of St. Lucy. The story connected to the purchase is a funny one. Phil Wood had the responsibility of looking for the property. It was realized that we had to think of somewhere not close to the Capital as this would be too expensive for our budget.

BARBADOS | 59

Phil knew this gentleman who owned land around the island and approached him. He was the one who did sell us the property. To begin with he gave us the locality and the price of the land. The Assembly liked both and agreed to the purchase.

When Phil told him the Assembly had agreed, the man paused, asked how many were on the Assembly. When Phil told him 9 people, the man, gasped, saying something like… "Good grief, man, how did 9 people ever agree?" Phil tried to explain the Bahá'í concept of consultation and unity but felt the man never did grasp the concept.

L to R: Jackie Stratton, Emily Kramer, Pat, Eve Johnson after nailing up the "This is our Temple property" sign in St. Lucy Parish.

One really memorable institute I remember was one weekend session run by Hazel Lovelace from Alaska. It was based solely on the verse of Bahá'u'lláh's which starts with "Intone o my servants the verses of God…" We went over and over and over that same verse for the whole two days!

At the end of the second day I was so full spiritually-speaking that my head felt like it was going to burst. I went into my room to rest. About 5 minutes later Hazel came into the room and said to me "Would you like to say some prayers?" I couldn't believe my ears! I looked at her and said, "Hazel if you open your mouth to start a prayer, I will hit you!"

To this day that verse is still burned into my memory!

It was here in Barbados that I first met Shamsi Sedeghat. She was a Persian Bahá'í who was currently pioneering in Trinidad. She was coming through the islands on a teaching trip and would arrive in Barbados shortly. I had been told by one of our Bahá'ís that she and I would clash and never get along. This is not a great way to look forward to meeting someone.

She arrived; we took one look at each other, recognized a kindred spirit and became immediate life-long friends. I loved that lady. She was a teacher of the Faith of the caliber that I had never experienced before except for Ruth Pringle. She was fearless, and always dealt with those of the so-called upper class. Appointments were made for her long before she came with as many high-ranking government persons and clergy as possible. She always carried a scrap book with her showing the other high-ranking persons from other places she had visited. It was an impressive group, from Ministers of both government and religions, and included Presidents and Ambassadors of countries.

Media was also alerted, and she was regularly on both radio and television once it arrived in the islands. Her interviews with the press always became an article in the local newspapers. In 1973 she also was able to obtain free Bahá'í radio programs which were still running in 1977.

I do hope someone gets her history down before she goes. Her record of service to the Faith is incredible. She told me her family had been asked by Shoghi Effendi to go to Cyprus. They were the first Bahá'ís into the country since the Covenant-breakers who included Mirza Yahya had been sent there in the summer of 1868 by the edict of Sultan 'Abdu'l-'Aziz. This edit also condemned Bahá'u'lláh to lifelong imprisonment in 'Akká, Israel.

This family was very strong. It would take a family of this caliber to withstand any negative effects left from covenant breakers. In later years she also served in Africa as the nurse to Hand of the Cause of God, Musa Banani.

When Frank was teaching at the school in Belleplaine one of his co-workers was a gentleman named Frank Fernandes. The two Franks got talking and as one would expect the Faith was brought up. The teacher was interested and asked to read something about the history of the Faith. My Frank came home and for a reason unclear to me at the time but was clearly guidance, took him the "Dawn Breakers". Now this is a book with several hundred pages, chilling events and some graphic photographs. It never, ever, would have been my first choice to give a new contact.

However, it turned out fine, not only was Frank F. still interested, he wanted us to meet and tell his cousin, Eve Fernandes as well. My Frank had already met her by a strange turn of events. He was hitchhiking, which was still safe and acceptable during that time frame. He was out on the road, sees a car coming, sticks out his thumb, then realizes it's a woman and not likely to stop. Later said she had never stopped to pick up men and she had her child in the car as well. But stop she did.

They got to chatting and she said her cousin Frank Fernandes worked at the same school as he did. I then met Eve and she and I hit it off and we became friends. Eventually I was giving her the same Bahá'í history outline that Maxine had used for me when she taught me. I figured it worked for me, why not her?

During the night session of our Bahá'í National Convention in 1974, I received a phone call from Eve saying she wanted to become a Bahá'í! Wow, "I will be right there" I said. I got to her home and her cousin Frank was there as well. I gave Eve her enrollment card which she signed right away. Frank says to me, "How about me, can't I join?" You bet you can, and he signed his card. I noticed two wine glasses on the table and felt I had to be sure they understood that alcohol was not allowed in the Faith. They both laughed and said, yes, they knew, they just had one last drink to celebrate their becoming Bahá'ís.

The three of us then traveled to the Bahá'í Centre where Convention was being held. They walked into the Centre in the most reverent way one can imagine, it was like they were floating. I was behind them, holding up their enrollment cards so all would see and know what had just happened. It was a wonderful thrilling event. Those two became such strong Bahá'ís. Eve became secretary of the National Assembly for years and Frank a strong active teacher of the Faith. To this day they still serve the Faith.

It was now getting time for us to leave the island. We could not get any more extensions as Grandma had died. No job had opened up, even though there was a big article in the local newspaper talking about the need for more Science and Math teachers needed in the school system.

We consulted with the National Assembly as we always did and asked if they had a preference as to which island we should try. They said that as Dominica had recently been added to this Bahá'í jurisdiction, he should try to get a position there.

Frank travelled there and was hired right away in the Catholic Secondary school as one of their teachers had gone away for further education.

It was done… We packed, but I did not want to leave Grandma with no one to visit her gravesite which was what she had feared. I appealed to the friends to:

Please do visit her once in a while.

We are now on our way to Dominica.

| 5 |

DOMINICA:
MARCH 1976 TO OCTOBER 1977

My first visit to Dominica was in the summer of 1969 when I had taken a teaching trip down the islands. I was very awed by the natural beauty of the island. It was relatively underdeveloped in comparison the other islands I had seen. It was so green and lush and quiet. By the end of the five days I stayed here it became my favorite island. But I try not to spread that opinion around to the other islands! Rúhíyyih Khánum after one of her visits there said it was one of the most beautiful places she had ever been…wow!

Another reason it became my favorite were the people. While generally speaking, I find West Indians are kind, honest, and open to new ideas and will give you a chance to prove yourself. Dominicans go a little further than that. A good example of what I mean by that was shown by the ladies who sell things in the open market. Usually on other islands I had to pay more for my goods than local people simply because I was a stranger, a white American and everyone thinks they are all rich. But there, I was charged the same as anyone else. It made me feel good to be seen as "One of us".

My second visit was in the summer of 1975. A teaching team of eight was formed with members from Barbados, St. Vincent and Dominica. It was composed of

Bahá'ís who were already friends so the trip was smooth and fun. One of the organized activities was a Bahá'í book display at the library. It drew a lot of attention with lots of material being given away and new friends of the Faith were made.

One of the people who enrolled during this project was a young man from a prominent Dominican family. It was really hoped that he would become deepened and serve the Faith and reach others at this level of society. Sadly, this did not happen; he became interested in politics and chose that path instead.

The team made a visit trip to the Carib Indian Reservation. It was very interesting for me. We also were able to present a Bahá'í book to the reservation leader, Mas Clem Frederick. But the most memorable to me was the visit of Hand of the Cause of God Enoch Olinga in March 1977 when he and his wife Elizabeth visited there. He gave his appearance as had been planned by the National Assembly. Afterwards I invited them to our home and they graciously accepted.

Presentation of The Proclamation of Bahá'u'lláh *to Mas Clam (centre), Carib Indian Chief, Dominica, by a teaching team under the direction of the National Spiritual Assembly of Barbados and the Windward Islands; August, 1975. Auxiliary Board member Shirley Yarbrough is seen on the extreme right.*
L to R: Yvette Clarke, Edirth Elcock, Pat Paccassi, Don Providence, Mas Clam, Mrs Clam, Mona George, and Shirley Yarbrough

Mr. Olinga and his wife Elizabeth's visit to our house in Dominica was charming. We lived in a small house on a big estate and it was all country. As we were all sitting in our screened porch, some

Visit of Hand of the Cause of God, Enoch Olinga (4th. from right) and Elizabeth Olinga, (1st. Right): to Dominica, 1977

chickens strolled by, and they both laughed, clapped their hands, saying, "It's just like home". Mr. Olinga made tea for us all, and as they were leaving, he turned to me and said, "I'll see you in Haifa next year". This sorta surprised Frank and I, as we had been the National Assembly together for many years, but we said nothing. Next year at our National Convention, I was elected to serve, but Frank was not, and I did see Mr. Olinga in Haifa, as we stayed at the same hotel!

One of life's ironies hit me right after we had moved here. Up until this time I had been regularly serving as the recording secretary for our National Assembly. We moved here in March 1976. In April I was once again on the National Assembly, but now elected as the Corresponding Secretary. Wow. This meant a whole set of different duties requiring a lot of time spent in the National Office in Barbados taking care of the Assembly's business. I now had to travel from Dominica to Barbados and stay there for two weeks every month. This was of course made so much more difficult as we lived on the opposite side of the island from the airport.

Another story that comes to mind even though it didn't happen during our stay there is an experience of one of the Dominican Bahá'ís. His name is Paul Von Elizee. He is a Carib Indian and one of the first who became Bahá'ís. His wife, Christaline, was the first Carib Indian to accept the Faith. They lived on the Reservation and had always attended the Catholic Church there.

One Sunday after he had enrolled, he was in Church and after the sermon, the Priest said to all, "I hear there is a Bahá'í with us today". GULP! This could not have been an easy moment for Paul. But God gives us strength and he stood up and said, "I am the one". The Priest nodded and still in front of the whole congregation asked Paul to come to his office after service.

During this meeting, Paul said the Priest was very cordial and only asked about the Faith. Paul then proceeded to tell him as best he could. Paul and Christaline remained strong Bahá'ís. Paul served on the 1982-83 National Spiritual Assembly of the Bahá'ís of the Windward Islands.

I have learned to love how Bahá'í quandaries are solved. They usually are, but not always how one expects. Our area was to receive a travel teacher of some renown, Meherangiz Munsiff. The National Assembly wanted to be able to prepare a proper agenda for her. No one knew what she looked like so how would we know to sight her when she arrived at the airport. I was set to travel to Barbados for my regular two weeks. I boarded the plane, saw an empty seat, sat down and there next to me was a lovely lady wearing a Sari. "Are you Mrs. Munsiff?" I asked. Of course she was. I introduced myself and we started to chat becoming good friends from that moment.

I did get a bit of a shock in a moment. The stewardess announced that our flight to Antigua would take approximately 40 minutes. What? Antigua, I was supposed to be on a plane to Barbados. The stewardess then spoke again explaining some plane had broken down or something and we were to pick up passengers in Antigua flying to Barbados. But it was fine with me; the dilemma on picking up Mrs. Munsiff was solved. You gotta love it!

There was a lovely young Bahá'í girl, Connie Didier, about Judy's age living close to us. The two of them became good friends and soon started to plan a teaching trip together to the island of Grenada. All went well and I proudly put the two of them on a plane to serve the Faith. This was her first teaching trip not with her Mother. I am sure one can imagine how very proud I was of my daughter!

In November of 1976 Al Segen and his sister, Edith Johnson, came to the island as pioneers. They moved to the capital, Roseau. This was good as we were on the other side of an island not easy to get around. They were wonderful people and experienced pioneers. Al was also a short-wave radio ham. This skill was a great help for this island as a category five Hurricane "David", hit there in fall of 1979. It was a devastating event; the island ran out of good water, food and was without electricity as well. Al, with his CB radio was able to communicate with the outside world. At a later date he was given a special award by Government for his dedicated services, as the island had been evacuated where Al stayed with other emergency personnel to give this service to the island.

In 1977 the teacher who had gone overseas for further training returned to Dominica. There were no other teaching jobs open for Frank. It was time to leave.

We again consulted with the National Assembly, asking them where they would like us to go. Its' first choice was St. Lucia. Except for Esther Evans, Knight of Bahá'u'lláh, for the Windward Islands, who was 78, there were no other pioneers on the island. Once on my way back from the two weeks in Barbados I stopped in St. Lucia on an errand for the Assembly. While there I picked up a St. Lucia *Gazette,* a government publication listing all the open teaching positions. I found that there were several openings for Science and Math teachers. Frank sent resumes to each school. As it turned out, all the resumes ended up in one place, the Teaching Service Commission.

A month after school had started the Commission called Frank and asked if he could teach Engineering Science. "Of course," he said. After the phone call he turned to me and said, "I wonder what Engineering Science is?" They had offered him a teaching position and we were on our way. Much to their surprise two weeks later we were in St. Lucia. They had not expected him until the start of the next term in January 1978 and this was only October 1977. Never mind, we were happy to be there. The Government put us in a guest house for several weeks where several people became Bahá'ís.

| 6 |

ST. LUCIA:
OCTOBER 1977 – MARCH 1990

Coming to St. Lucia gave us a wonderful chance to get to know Esther Evans. She was a Knight of Bahá'u'lláh for the Windward Islands. She came in October 1954 with another Bahá'í woman, Lillian Middlemast, who however, had to leave the next year. This left Esther by herself, but it did not deter her at all. What a great lady she was, charming, gracious and totally dedicated to the Faith. Her story is remarkable. There were three interviews with her which I consolidated into one, bringing all this information we had about her from the interviews into one document. This is a link to it: http://www.bahaihistorycaribbean.info/A_Chat_with_Esther_Evans.pdf

I love this photo of her with Rúhíyyih Khánum taken in June 1970.

L to R: Violette Nakhjavání, Martha Hocker, Esther and Amatu'l-Bahá Rúhíyyih Khánum.

St. Lucia has been blessed with many visits of Hands of the Cause of God. Each of their visits was memorable. Before they came, the friends and institutions were galvanized into action arranging for their activities. While on the island everyone was anxious to be part of the planned activities. Visits were arranged to communities not visited in a while. I, who was not working and had a car, was asked to drive them. Wow! What a bounty. But I am still embarrassed by the memories of them driving around in that old beat-up car we had. But none of them ever complained.

One drive I remember well is when Mr. Khadem visited. Ruth Pringle, our Counsellor was here as well. I had traveled many roads together with her before in service to the Faith. However, I was not particularly known for having cautious, slow driving skills. Indeed, the youth in the back of the van would chant "Go, granny, go". But when driving a Hand of the Cause of God, one changes one's style. Ruth and I picked up Mr. Khadem at the airport and drove him to his hotel. I had adopted my "Hand" style of driving and when we arrived at the hotel, Mr. Khadem commented "You are such a wonderful safe driver", Ruth gave me a look that shouted "huh"; but she didn't give me away. I love Ruth Pringle.

This photo shows Mr. Khadem, Ruth, Esther and I at National Convention in 1983.

It should be explained here that as Frank was hired while on another island, he was officially listed as an overseas teacher. This entitled him to government housing and a bonus once a year. At the time the bonus seemed great, however in the end it meant that he was not being given a pension which local teachers are entitled to and that meant we would have no financial support on St. Lucia after he retired. This is what precipitated the move to Trinidad twelve years later. A fuller explanation of this comes at a later point in the story.

As the government had not expected us so early, there was not any housing available at that time. They put us in a guest house, Planters Inn, in the middle of Castries. It was also right across from the Catholic Church which ran its bells at all hours from early morning on; oh my, that takes a bit of getting used to. We were able to teach the Faith to lots of new persons while staying there and those who lived at the guest house did become Bahá'ís.

We were eventually moved to a nice house in an area called Sans Souci. It was quiet, sort of safe and close to the town area. I say "Sort of safe" in that we did have two break-ins at the house.

The first one was when I had been in town shopping and arrived home to see the back door open. OH, OH, not good. I stepped carefully inside and coming down the hallway carrying one of my pillowcases full of my goodies is a "Thief". We both moved slowly to the living room facing one another.

I wasn't sure what the best thing was to do. However, I somehow remembered that very recently Karate movies had been introduced on the island. Every kid you saw was practicing moves. I saw out of the corner of my eye my broom leaning against the wall. I ran to get it, took the stick part in my two hands, jumped forward at him and shouted, "Ah hah!" His eyes got big, his mouth dropped open and you could see he was not at all sure what this crazy white woman was going to do to him. He took the best action he could probably think of; he dropped the pillowcase and ran like the thief he was.

The second one did not turn out as nicely. This thief came and was gone by the time I got home. He took all the jewelry he could find. This included my Grandma's Bahá'í ring. That was not nice! This ring had originally been made for me by my spiritual mother, Maxine Roth and given to me during one of my trips to see her in Colombia where she was a pioneer. When I got home, I went to show off my new ring to Grandma. Her face lit up, she slipped it on her finger, saying "Oh this is so pretty". OK, what would you have done? Probably the same as I did. I said "You can have this ring Grandma; I see you love it so much already"; and she wore it happily ever after. It's no wonder I hated so much to lose such a precious item as this ring. I confess, I did not wish that thief a smooth life.

Actually, there was a small third robbery at this house. One night the friends were gathered for a Bahá'í meeting and I had baked a cake. It was sitting in the kitchen cooling before being frosted. After a bit I went into the kitchen to frost the cake parts that had been cooling on separate plates. I looked and lo and behold only one plate of cake there. Wow, where did the other half go? We came to the conclusion that a thief must have smelled the cake, took a peek through the open door, helped himself, but graciously decided to share and left us one half of the cake!

In January 1978, the National Assembly received notice that a Jamaican Bahá'í, Beverly March was coming to our area as a pioneer. This is great news! After consultation it was decided that she should go to St. Lucia. More great news, she is to stay with us. Working with local Bahá'ís is always an asset if not close to a necessity. She was also close to Judy's age, even better. She arrived in January of 1978 and stayed until 1981.

Beverly was a schoolteacher and obtained a job teaching in a secondary school close to where we lived. She had a great outgoing personality and attracted people wherever she went and everyone she met, sooner or later, was taught the Bahá'í Faith. She ended up bringing several Bahá'ís into the Faith. Probably the most notable contact she made was Moses Henry. It was she who started his enrollment. She had hitched a ride from him one day when returning from one of the villages. It was still safe to do that in those days. At any rate, she, of course, started to tell him about the Faith and ended up giving him a Bahá'í book.

He later tells the story of how the book sat on his shelf for a long time. One day, he said, the book seemed to call him. He took it down, started reading and realized right away he had to get in touch with the Bahá'ís. He had heard that there Bahá'ís living in Gros Islet, drove right out there, found Marjorie and Larry Clarke who were pioneers, just as they were about to leave this village to go to another one on the island. They referred him to Stephanie Bloodworth who lived closer to him.

This is Marjorie Clarkes' story of Moses Henry's enrollment:

> "The day we moved from Gros Islet to Castries we moved our few possessions out to the green van while we finished cleaning. Larry and I were busy scrubbing the last room in our second-floor apartment, about to lock up, when there was a knock on the door. A man we had never seen

before stood at the top of the stairs, out of breath, and asked, "Is this the Bahá'í bookstore?"

"No, but we are Bahá'ís," and we introduced ourselves. He wanted to know if we had any books he could buy. The only things left in the apartment were a mop, a scrub pail and a plastic bag of books belonging to the LSA! So we offered to lend him two books and he gave us his address so we could retrieve them in two weeks' time. We were happy to find that he lived just around the corner from the Paccassi family in Castries.

Moses Henry was his name and he had given a ride to a young Bahá'í pioneer ten years before. We never met her, but I think she was African American or West Indian and pioneered elsewhere in the Caribbean. [Pat's note: this was Beverly March from Jamaica]

She had given him a leaflet about the Faith, and he'd remembered it all this time. After a brief conversation Moses left and I ran over to the window to look down on the street. "Larry, he is driving away!" I accented the driving part since there were almost no cars owned by Bahá'ís in those days.

Two weeks later Stephanie Bloodworth and I went to his home to get the books. Moses greeted us and invited us in. I remember that his home seemed full of various young relatives who seemed to be students. One of them served us juice and made us welcome.

There was a very positive conversation about what Moses had learned from the books. Then he asked if he could make a contribution to the Bahá'í Fund. Stephanie thanked him for the offer but explained that only Bahá'ís could contribute to the Fund. Moses said that, in that case, he would like to be a member and what did he need to do to enroll as a Bahá'í? I remember exchanging glances with Stephanie - after all, who had ever heard of someone enrolling so that they could give a donation to the Fund?

From that day forward Moses was a devoted member of the Bahá'í community of St. Lucia."

Beverly and I put a lot of miles on our old-run-down car traveling to the villages around the island. One trip however stands out in my mind. It was getting dark and we were going up a steep hill next to a Ravine. It had rained, the roads were slippery, and the brakes were not working properly. They would slip and we would slide backwards and sideways. I was driving and it was nerve-wracking, made ever so worse by Beverly being extremely nervous. When Bev was nervous, she laughed, a high shrill laugh and she couldn't stop doing it. Even now, I'm not sure what was worse, sliding around this hill or listening to her maniacal laugh.

Bev and I have remained good friends and to this day we both consider her my "Jamaican daughter". She tells everyone we are her pioneering parents.

One time while still living in Sans Souci we received an enrollment card of a new Bahá'í youth named Juliana Auguste. She lived in the capital town of Castries but had been visiting friends in one of the villages. A Bahá'í travel teacher was there and had attracted a crowd on the road. Juliana listened and signed her Bahá'í card right there. We went looking for her, found the house and invited her to our house for further study.

She arrived the next Sunday with her younger brother Moses. Bev and I then started the youth classes. We would study, then Bev would teach Juliana embroidery and I gave guitar lessons to Moses. I was the proud owner of a guitar given to me by a travel teacher. I taught Moses every note and chord I knew: C F G and for fancy stuff, D minor. I did not find out until years later that their older brother Denis had brought them to the classes and stayed outside the house "Just in case".

Moses progressed very quickly on the guitar and I ended up letting him take it home to practice. He got so good he ended up being able to earn his living at it.

These two, Juliana and Moses remained Bahá'ís. Later when we had moved to our next house at Vigie, there was a nice little group of youth consisting of their cousin and some friends. We studied the book "Release the Sun" every Sunday. We did not have to give crafts anymore, but we had a ping pong table downstairs which they loved. By this time Denis no longer had to bring them.

A lot of interesting and instructive things happened in the Sans Souci house.

By this time Lynn had finished high school in the United States, married Richard Berry and had a son Ian. They also were now pioneers in St. Croix in the U.S. Virgin Islands. Rick had a job as a factory manager but for some reason was not happy with it. During a visit to St. Lucia they met one of our new Bahá'ís, Lennox Jerome, who owned a business and he grandly told Rick "You should come work for me".

Unfortunately, Rick had not been in the Caribbean long enough to be able to separate politeness with genuineness. Rick quit his job in St. Croix, moved the family to St. Lucia expecting that a job was waiting here for him.

Lennox, the new Bahá'í, was gracious about it; he let Rick come to the office. But it became clear that there really was no opening for him at all. So they were now living with us in Sans Souci.

The month before Lynn and Rick arrived, a young family from Canada, Keith and Stephanie Bloodworth and their 9-month-old son Rúhu'lláh, came to St. Lucia to pioneer.

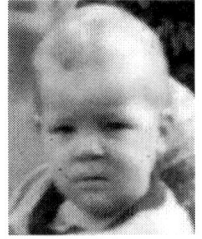

I had first met Steph at Planters Inn in Castries when she came on a teaching trip. She was young, pretty and pregnant. The National Assembly wanted a male companion for Frank Fernandes from Barbados who at this point was travel teaching and working in Vieux Fort. But Keith couldn't come so he sent Steph instead.

I put her on the plane to Vieux Fort for the 20-minute ride and Frank met her at the airport. It wasn't more than 5 minutes after she got there that I got a phone call from Stephanie. "Hello" she says slowly and sweetly, "This is Steph calling. I um, am not really sure but, um, Frank here says I should stay with him in the house he rented. Now maybe, um, they are different here, but um, in Canada it would not at all be proper for me to stay with him alone in the house." "What, of course it's not proper!" I said, "Put Frank on the phone". I had soon straightened out that little issue and they did end up being a good teaching team but not staying in the same house. Those two are some of the best teachers of the Faith that I have had the pleasure to know.

It was from this teaching trip that the Bloodworth's had decided to pioneer here. What a bounty for our island. However they had not gotten jobs yet, so they stayed with us for a while in Sans Souci at the same time as Lynn and Rick and son Ian.

So we have now grown to 10 in the house including two boys under a year old. In spite of my loving each and every one of them I must confess at this point that I was not all together thrilled at so many in the house at one time. We also had been informed that a travel teacher, Jaitun Abdul from Trinidad, was arriving and would we please pick her up. I had made her a reservation in a modest guest house near us and invited her to lunch at our house first. She is lovely and charming. She walks into the house, chooses a chair, sits down and states "When you got a place to sit, you got a place to sleep." OK, now we are 11 in the house. And I gain another lifetime friend.

By this time Emily Kramer had moved from Barbados to St. Lucia. She did live at the other end of the island but was a frequent visitor to the house. It was in this time frame that the story of her "tires" took place. This story will be told during the second St. Lucia visit.

We had a fellow from the countryside who took care of our yard. He was steady, polite and cheerful. A few years later after we had moved and no longer needed a gardener, I read in the paper that he and two others were to be hanged for murdering someone. Wow!

In November of 1978 our spiritual Father, Wayne Hoover and Paul Rourke came to St. Lucia on their teaching trip through the Islands. Wayne had cancer but seemed to be able to function very well with all the meds he took. Several meetings and media events were planned. Wayne with his usual style charmed everyone he met, and he was a dramatic Bahá'í teacher.

On one of the previous islands Wayne had scratched his throat on one of the crushed meds he was taking. This turned out to be a fatal blow to him as his throat became infected and he was not well enough to fight off the infection. He died in our home on 10 November 1978 and is buried in Choc Cemetery, in a beautiful spot next to the Caribbean Sea. Our Knight of Bahá'u'lláh Esther Evans graciously allowed him to be buried in her plot.

As land on the islands is in not inexhaustible many cemetery plots are built to hold more than one person. When Esther died and was buried in her tomb big enough for three persons, the quiet joke among the Bahá'ís from overseas was "I wonder if it's all right for Wayne and Esther to be sleeping together?"

By now the government finally had one of their houses available for us to move into. It was in the area called Vigie as it overlooked the Vigie Airport with the Caribbean Sea right next to the airstrip. I loved the house and the view. It was built of Green Heart, a wood which is extremely strong, and thus termite resistant, an important element in tropical dwellings. It also had a lovely porch facing the sea. It was on this porch that I strengthened my self-control. I was here to serve the Faith, not sit on this lovely porch, enjoying the breeze and the beautiful view.

Lynn, Rick, and Ian moved to this house with us. Their second son, Sean was born while we all lived in this house in Vigie. Sean still has citizenship status on St. Lucia if he cared to utilize it.

Bev and Sean

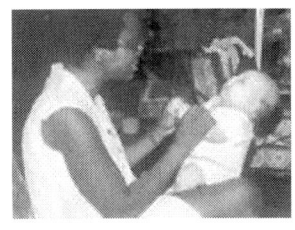

Our porch overlooked the airport with a departure schedule that needed getting used to. Every morning at 6 am a crop duster took off to go to work. If you haven't heard a crop duster airplane, it's hard to imagine the roaring sound of its engine as it lifts off the ground. But as all things must, we adjusted to the sound and when travel teachers would stay with us and ask, "How can you stand that noise?" We would look blankly and say, "What noise?"

Both Stephanie Bloodworth and Beverly March and myself loved giving children's classes. By December 1978 we had five active classes and my youth group going as well. Steph and I taught a class in one of the smaller villages in St. Lucia. We would take the van and travel there once a week. As we started on the road to the village itself, we could see streams of children running down the hill to attend the classes. They also were trying to catch us soon enough so that they could ride the rest of the way in the van with us. They counted that as a real treat.

We were never able to have a proper meeting place in the village. We would hold most of the classes inside an abandoned dilapidated house with holes in the floors big enough to get your whole foot caught. But the children loved the classes, and if they didn't mind the venue neither did we. One of the local Bahá'ís there told me one time that we were the only ones who had ever tried to do something for their children.

In Guyana in 1978 followers of the Peoples Temple cult leader, Jim Jones, committed mass suicide by drinking poisoned Kool-Aid. Over 900 people died at that time. An interesting anecdote that arose in our community from the aftermath of that news is as follows.

As one might imagine the poisoning was all the talk in our area! Years later I heard a story when I was doing interviews with those who had been in my youth class at Vigie during that time frame. I was told that the youth group had consulted among themselves as to what they should do. No one wanted to stop coming to the classes, but one should take precautions Who knows if we would sometime try to get them to do something like that and we did serve Kool Aid. The eventual plan they came up with was to stop accepting anything to eat or drink and one of them should always be seated near the door. That way, one of them could always escape and go for help if necessary. In the end when I heard the plan, I thought it was a pretty good plan; good for them! Fortunately, their fears eventually went away, and they once again felt safe with us.

In 1979 I was "up" for the award for holding the most National Committee positions in one Bahá'í year; they numbered 6; Public Relations Officer, Photographer, Property Committee, Children's Committee, Librarian and Correspondence Course.

This was also the year I was appointed by the National Assembly to represent the Bahá'í Faith on the National Council of Women's Voluntary Organizations. This group was composed of representatives of all the religions in St. Lucia. I had originally met with them in order to inform them of the Bahá'í religious presence on the island. The women on the Council were all dedicated and hardworking individuals.

The President of the Council was Heraldine Rock. Mrs. Rock was an amazing woman, multi-talented, hardworking and persistent. Nothing was too hard for her to tackle, including the then male dominated field of politics. She stood for the government office of representative of an area and was vigorously opposed, including someone trying to burn her house down to discourage her. However, she did win the seat. Mrs. Rock is the 3rd from the left in the photo.

I was soon elected secretary of the Council, so she, who was its chairman, and I worked closely together and became the best of friends.

Her work for the betterment of the condition and the rights of women in the country was legendary. This council established the first "Crisis Centre for

Women". It also was among the first to honour women for their contributions to the nation. An award ceremony was held at the Official Residence of the Prime Minister who also presented the trophies. 25 outstanding women were chosen from varied fields and received trophies. I do have to mention that the officers of the Council were honoured at this ceremony and my trophy sits nicely on the bookcase.

I think, to me, the funniest thing she ever did was her action taken at a waterfront confrontation with the men who were to be loading hers and other banana growers crop onto a Geest ship bound for sale in the United Kingdom. The men were striking and would not load the bananas. She soon got tired of this and picked up a stalk of bananas, put it on the top of her head and started up the gangplank. The other women on the dock were now galvanized. They all picked up bananas and followed her up the gangplank. Oops, the men now realized if the women could and would do it, they might be out of work and they quickly grabbed bananas themselves and went up behind the women.

The following year Prince Phillip visited the island and during his visit met her. Ah, he said, smiling broadly, you are the lady who broke the Geest strike.

Her overall work was recognized officially by the St. Lucian government and in the end one of three newly built buildings in the capital was named for her. Wow, see what can happen when one goes pioneering; I have never before or since even met a person who had a building named after them.

She also received an OBE. An OBE is a British Queen's honour given to an individual for a major local role in any activity such as business, charity or the public sector. OBE stands for Officer of the Most Excellent Order of the British Empire.

By October of 1979 it had become clear that Rick would not be able to get work on St. Lucia. Even with their second son, Sean, who was a St. Lucia citizen, did not help their chances of staying on the island. They decided to go to Grenada which needed pioneers. They remained there until 1983 when they returned to the United States. It was years later on their second pioneering move that they again came to the area as pioneers to St. Thomas. Richard died there in 2016 from a heart attack. Lynn now serves at the Bahá'í World Centre in Haifa, Israel.

However, their move to Grenada was hard for me. I had grown so fond of my newly-known grandsons. It was with a heavy heart as I watched them going down the stairs on their way to the airport. But at the bottom of the stairs, Ruhi, the oldest son of the Bloodworth's looked up at me and said, "I'll be back soon gramma". He had never called me that before! Wow, I still had a grandson living on the island.

We now had to leave our government housing at Vigie as Frank's contract was up and he had been re-hired on St. Lucia, so he was no longer able to receive the perks of the overseas teacher. I began to look for a house, and seemed much to my puzzlement, driving up the same road in an area I had no interest living in. But I did find a house around there and we moved. After we had moved in, I began to become uncomfortable in this house. So I began once again to drive up this same road looking for another place to live. One day I turned a corner and there was a house almost like the one we had at Vigie, and there was a for rent sign in front. Hurrah!

We moved and soon discovered that Moses Henry lived just a few houses away from us. Oh my, you gotta love it when a plan comes together. We became great friends and continued the process of his deepening. Moses ended up performing great services for the Faith. He served as the secretary of the National Spiritual Assembly for a number of years. The photo shows Frank, Mama Bahá'í, Moses and Gregory Robinson out in one of the villages.

Moses was also a wonderful teacher of the Faith. If you travelled anywhere with him, you best not be in a hurry. He had built the roads in St. Lucia and knew everyone, everywhere. So no matter where you travelled, he would find someone to stop and talk to about the Faith.

A word here about a blessing for St. Lucia was the presence of Mama Bahá'í. In 1979 she came to our area as a pioneer, staying until 1984 living in Guadeloupe. She participated as a team member for the Grandma Snyder teaching project held in 1981. Mama Bahá'í was a descendant of Mírzá Muḥammad-Qulí, the faithful half-brother and companion in exile of Bahá'u'lláh.

To have a Bahá'í who was a member of the Holy Family as a pioneer was a bounty for the whole area. She was on the project team with Stephanie Bloodworth. I can still see the two them walking hand in hand up a road in the area where we were teaching the Faith. It was on this road they met and enrolled Cadosia DuBoulay who to this day has remained strong and steadfast, still serving on the National Assembly.

She told me the story of how her family got their last name. The family was living in Haifa. One day she was with 'Abdu'l-Bahá and asked him why she didn't have a last name like all the children did here. She said he smiled at her and said of course you do, it's Baha'i. From that time on the family carried that precious name as their last name.

In November of 1980 we had our first Bahá'í wedding. Tim and Helen Delphus who had been brought into the Faith by Steph had become firm believers and wanted to formalize their union. At that time, the National Assembly did not have the authority to legally perform weddings in the country. It was arranged for me to take them to a government office where the legal ceremony could be held. The Bahá'í ceremony took place at Esther Evans home that evening.

When I picked them up to go for the government ceremony I had to smile. Helen was wearing her hair in curlers and Tim in a T-Shirt and pants. They knew which ceremony was the real one! They have remained strong devoted Bahá'ís.

For me, the really memorable event held on the island was the Grandma Snyder Teaching Project. It was summer of 1981 when Steph came to me with an idea she had in a dream. This was the source of this project! Steph had never met my Grandma but of course I had told her lots about her. I was also enthusiastic about the idea. We took it to the National Assembly who approved it and began the planning stage. I was appointed as the coordinator. We knew it had to be an international team effort. This was the time frame in which teaching projects were in progress everywhere, so it was easy to get people to come to St. Lucia and participate. The photo below reflects the diversity of this beautiful team.

L to R: Steve Horn, Pat Paccassi, Edith Johnson, Helen Delphus, Alison Vacarro, Sara Jane Lee, Keith Bloodworth, Moses Auguste, Russell Lee, Julien Alphonse, James Auguste, Richard Berry, Frank Paccassi, Child, Badi Bloodworth, Stephanie Bloodworth, Shirley Yarbrough. Kneeling: Sammy Delphus, Susan Felker, Juliana Auguste, Nancy Cole, Soraya Golbarani.

Small Insert showing the St. Lucian teachers: ____, ____, Helen Delphus, Sammy Delphus, Moses Auguste, Julien Alphonse, Juliana Auguste, Martin Devaux, ____.

The project was set for 27 July to 17 August. Teachers arrived from everywhere. An extensive orientation was given, and teams set. The teams were to cover the entire island having certain villages chosen as teaching sites. St. Lucians were asked to be the team captains. Children's classes were started during the project. There was a huge response; the classes were fun, "outsiders" were always an attraction and it was summertime, all the children were out of school.

It was a great project. Everyone got along so well and were enthusiastic teachers of the Faith. It also was a good time frame for introducing a new religion in the country. St. Lucia has been predominately a Catholic nation. To give a good example of their influence, when the government first decided to bring legalized gambling into the country, the Church was very much against it and urged everyone to take to the streets in a protest and it brought thousands to the streets and the government had to back down.

But now people were open to changes. The Bahá'í teachings and principles were very attractive to St. Lucians and they embraced the Faith in large numbers. The stories coming from this project were wonderful and inspiring.

The National Spiritual Assembly did everything it could to help these large numbers of new Bahá'ís to become deepened. Conferences were held. As many visits as possible to each area were made. 500 newsletters were published each month, collated and mailed. It sounds like a lot of work and it was, but it was also fun and a chance for a lot of us to get together and serve the Faith as well.

Unfortunately, it wasn't enough, there were too many factors lacking. No local places to meet were available to us and we could not afford to build any. The concept that the followers were to be in charge and help was totally alien, everyone knows that is the job of the ministers. There were not enough people for good and productive follow up visits to all the areas.

Hindsight is always good of course, but it probably would have been more productive to teach and concentrate in one area and then move to another one at a later date. Oh my!

One of the other problems created was that with so many Bahá'ís in so many areas at Riḍván, Local Spiritual Assemblies had to be elected. The first year was not such a problem. The following years were. By that time, there was very little interest left so we had to help with the process of electing the assemblies. Frank and Keith became our "speed team". On 21 April, they hopped into the van, drove to all the relevant areas, found some of the believers, had them vote to form the Assembly and promptly drove to the next village to do the same thing.

It was not until later when the Universal House of Justice said that from now on, an area had to elect its Local Spiritual Assembly on its own. This reduced the number of assemblies drastically, but when they elected their own assembly, they functioned.

One of the fun things that happened was as a result of our mailing of so many newsletters to so many villages in the island. Steph and I got talking about it one day and we decided what we would do is drive around the island to every post office with a small gift for the postmaster/mistress for their trouble and cooperation. As there were lots of post offices the gift could not be anything expensive. It was at about the time when apples from the United States were first brought in into the country and were a huge success. I saw a man I knew spend money he was supposed to use to get something for his child buy an apple for himself instead.

We figured how many apples we would need, bought them and set out on our journey to all post offices in the country. I don't remember the number, but it was substantial. When we made our little presentation, the responses were really varied. Most thought it amusing but were happy to get the apple. The most memorable presentation was to a gentleman in his mid-50's, well dressed as a businessman and was most courteous. After we explained what we were there for, he got up from his chair, put on his suit coat, straightened his tie and graciously accepted our little gift!

By August of 1983 we now had eight active children's classes and a

Children's Conference was held in an area called the Morne. There were children present from nine communities around the island. The venue was on a hilltop with a large meeting hall. Each class had prepared a presentation and short classes were given. All went smoothly while inside the building. Afterwards, outside, it was a different story. Imagine that many children now free from being inside and fortified with sugar-filled refreshments running around without enough adults to properly supervise everyone's movements and activities.

When we got home that night, Steph and I were thrilled. We went on and on about how great it was. Frank and Keith who had been there helping were trying, very hard, not to groan.

In 1985 our youngest daughter, Judy had a serious mental illness come upon her. She did get some help here, but it became obvious that she would need more extensive help and support. We decided to take her back to the Carmichael, Sacramento, California area. She was eventually enrolled with an agency that was able to provide her with the full time help she needed. Bahá'u'lláh takes care of His own!

Many years later when we were living in Trinidad, she had a serious setback. We decided to go and help her through this period and remain with her in the U.S. if necessary. After she was better and once again settled, it was her choice that we not remain there with her so we returned to Trinidad to continue our pioneering efforts.

In the mid-eighties an endeavor called "The Bahá'í Encyclopedia Project" was commissioned by the Universal House of Justice. The National Spiritual Assemblies in our area were contacted and asked to submit articles with an historical prospective. Each of the islands, except for St. Lucia where John Kolstoe, a published author, lived, asked me to write the articles. It was a challenging endeavor, but lots of fun, digging through all the material I had already gathered. The articles I did were done in the mid-nineties and sent to project managers. The project was eventually put online, but in a much-reduced manner than had been originally thought, and did not include these historical articles. I will insert my articles onto my Baha'i historical web site.

This is link to the articles on my web site:

http://www.bahaihistorycaribbean.info/photo_galleries_and_more/island-history-articles/

This coming story ended in Trinidad, but it had a lot of action in St. Lucia, so I am telling it here. I call it "The Bowling Ball" story. It really doesn't have anything to do with pioneering as such, but in one way it does. I'll tell it and let you judge.

When we left California in 1965 with our worldly goods, for some reason, my bowling ball was packed as well. It's not that I was such a good bowler. I did belong to a woman's league, but it was for fun and my average was only 138. Not too shabby for a "girl", but still not really memorable, but the ball did have my name on it. It travelled all the previous islands with us into St. Lucia. None of them including St. Lucia had a bowling alley, but that didn't seem to bother me, and it was brought with us for every change of island.

One day in St. Lucia after we had been there for several years, I decided to get rid of the ball. We were then living in Ciceron. I didn't want to just "throw" it away. I decided I would put it out at the top of our driveway, knowing that it wouldn't be long before someone picked it up. A little while later I looked out and sure enough, it was gone. Later that day, I drove up to the gas station at the top of our hill. The manager came right over to me and said "Oh Miss Pat, I saw the man who took your ball and I got it back for you. Wait a minute I'll go get it."

Alright, it's now back with me. I thought a bit and thought we are never going to live where there is a bowling alley again. I needed to get rid of it. I wrapped it up, got in the car and found a dumpster and dumped the ball in it. Whew, it's now gone.

During our time in Sacramento, California with Judy, we became good friends with Charyl and Keith Thorpe. They had been pioneering in Trinidad and still owned a house there. During one of our talks Charyl said to me in effect that as we had no job in St. Lucia and no income except for our Social Security, why didn't we move to Trinidad and live in their house, rent free. There were also two apartments downstairs renting and we could use the income to maintain the property and ourselves. Wow, talk about an offer you couldn't refuse!

So in 1990 we were again moving, this time to Trinidad. Everything once again was packed up and shipped. We moved to the Thorpe's house and settled in.

We needed to get groceries and some supplies. We drove to a big mall; we parked, walked in the main door and the first thing that hit my eye was a "Bowling Alley". Somewhere, someone was having a good laugh on me. Our Trinidad chapter had begun.

| 7 |

TRINIDAD AND TOBAGO: 1990-2000

Coming to Trinidad, I thought, would be like or at least follow the patterns set up by our other island moves. This however was not the case. For the first time it was just Frank and I. No Judy, Lynn, Grandma or even our dog Robbie. We did of course come with our worldly possessions including the 35 boxes of books, but we always travelled with those.

Usually we had to make our own way, but here, we were picked up at the airport by a young Bahá'í, Ashmeed Edoo. We had met him before at the Thorpe's house in Roseville, California where he had been visiting them. Ashmeed is a wonderful man, a strong Bahá'í and a good friend to have.

My first impression of the island was being impressed with the long straight highways. Trinidad is 50 x 37 miles, St. Lucia is 27 x 14, Barbados is 21 x 14, and St. Thomas is 14 x 3.

He took us to the Thorpe's house which was situated in La Romain which is in the Southern part of the country. It was also in the same Bahá'í Community as Ashmeed. It was a lovely, large house with a view of the sea from the porch.

Over the years I found that this culture was very different than the other islands I had served on. One the main factors for this was the makeup of the background of the people. 40% were of African descent and 40% East Indian descent with the remaining 20% being European, Middle Easterners, Chinese, and mixtures thereof. This meant that traditions varied, such as weddings and funerals. One thing though, as Trinidadians became Bahá'ís they easily changed. The photos of a Bahá'í wedding and a Hindu wedding shown below give an excellent example:

Phillip and Lynn Heeralal

Funerals though gave us a start. The first one we attended was for a great Bahá'í, Ramkay Ramjattan. All was the same until the last of the funeral and they began to cover up the coffin with dirt while we were still there. Frank and I looked at each other, thinking "what is this?" Neither of us had seen a casket lowered into the ground before. Our experience was that the funeral ended before the casket was put into the ground.

Another funeral we attended was also of a Bahá'í. A member of one of the families rushed up to me and quietly asked "Which direction should the feet face?" Fortunately, I had just recently read the relevant passage from the Bahá'í Writings on this subject.

This was also the first time I had seen a shop selling "Bake and Shark"

The steel pan was a musical instrument I had never seen before. I loved it, has a great sound!

This photo was taken on our front porch.

Another example of culture differences for me with my North American background is in the local expressions in all of the islands we had lived in. Two examples:

    1. "I wouldn't mind".

This means "I would like to do this". But the expression itself can be taken in different ways, and also not understood. A good example of this happened during one of my trips to Haifa, Israel at the Bahá'í World Centre. I was waiting for the other Bahá'ís when a young Persian man came flying by me. He glanced at me, saw an older lady, and came to a sliding stop. He said to me "I am giving a ride in my car to a few Bahá'ís up to the next meeting. Would you like to come with us?" This meant a lovely drive instead of a hard climb up a steep hill. I said to him "I wouldn't mind". His eyeballs sorta rolled in his head. He knew what the words meant, but not their meaning. I saw this and promptly said "That would be very nice, thank you." He beamed, told me where to wait and was gone.

    2. "Just now".

This can be a very deceptive phrase. One eventually comes to realize what it means; certainly not now, maybe not in an hour, but sometime today.

Another big change for me in Trinidad was the number of active local believers. The other islands always had a solid but small core of local Bahá'ís. Here there were many from both East Indian and African backgrounds and taking part in the activities of the Faith. This was great.

The only thing I could see that was not, in my opinion, not as balanced as it should be dealt with Bahá'í Administration. With the large number of capable local Bahá'ís I was surprised that weren't more local Bahá'ís on the National

Spiritual Assembly. Instead there were five Persian pioneers. It did take a while for this to change, but it did change and Ashmeed Edoo was the first new one who was elected to the National Assembly which in turn led to a National Assembly with a majority of Trinidadian Bahá'ís on it.

A good example of the caliber of the Trinidadian Bahá'ís were the awards given by government to two local believers, Dr. Harry Collymore and Mansingh Amarsingh in 1999. It was a special meeting with the awards being presented by the President of Trinidad and Tobago, Noor Hasanali. Dr Collymore received the Trinity Cross (the highest award) for community service and Mansingh Amarsingh the Hummingbird medal for sports.

Our first ride in one of the local transportation options were taxis which ran regularly on the roads. You went out on the road, waited until one came, flagged it down, and you were on your way. The first one we got into, the driver turned around and stated "See, I have straight hair just like yours." As I found out later there was still a sense of division between the two dominant backgrounds. This extended into marriage, neighborhoods, friendships and the political realm. It has, however, gotten better over the years and as far as I could tell did not extend into the Bahá'í community.

Our first visitors were Dr. Fereydoon and Mrs. Marouk Rahimi. They were Persian pioneers in the country and lived in the same Bahá'í community as we now did. They brought us a gift of a luscious looking watermelon. Dr. Rahimi also came with a request from the National Assembly that I serve on the National Teaching Committee and the Institute Board. What was he saying! Remember I am now 71 years old; have just participated in the packing up of our house and the move to Trinidad including all the arrangements that such a move involves. I knew how much work a National Teaching Committee involved but wasn't sure of the Institute Board, whatever that was. Politely as I could I asked to be able to rest up a bit before jumping into Bahá'í activities such as those he was requesting. His wife agreed with me, and that started our friendship.

One of the first things that we did was to meet with the National Spiritual Assembly. The National Bahá'í Centre was in North of the country, in the capital city of Port of Spain. As we entered into the meeting room, the members of the National Assembly stood up to greet us. Boy, I was seriously impressed. I remember thinking this is a classy National Assembly. The gesture has remained with me

After we had more or less settled in, I decided not to accept the appointment to the National Teaching Committee but to work with the National Institute Board of Directors of Trinidad and Tobago. I had gotten more information on the work of this Board. I felt sure this was a solution to the follow up we had been looking for after the Mass Teaching period.

I attended my first meeting at Ann Marie and Ganesh (Bobby) Ramsahai's home who lived in the north-east of the island. I began to realize this island was going to mean a lot more travelling up and down in the country for me.

I was promptly elected the secretary…oh my, sure glad I rested up a bit first! Bobby who was the Auxiliary Board Member joined the Board at a later date.

While other personnel did change a bit, I remained on it until we left Trinidad.

L to R: Pat Paccassi, Kathy Farabi, Marouk Rahimi, Ann Marie Ramsahai. As you see this was a real diverse group, American, British, Persian and Trinidadian. It was a joy to work with them.

The Institute Process here was a lot further along than it had been in St. Lucia. We now started having the residential nine-day institutes covering both Book 1, Reflections on the Life of the Spirit and Book 3, Teaching Children's Classes.

As we lived in this big house it followed that the institutes

were held there. One of the institutes had 18 attendees. Others were smaller.

Frank was not involved with the institute process per se but was always very supportive. He would remain in the back during sessions and appear during break times. The boys who attended loved Frank. When he was in the back on the computer, they would all flock back there to see what he was doing. One time, as they were there, he somehow popped into an adults only site and naked women jumped onto the screen. I'm not sure who was more surprised, but I sure know Frank was more mortified. I suspect the boys didn't mind at all.

While all the institutes to me were great, some always stand out. However, one ended with a negative feeling that wasn't so great. In Trinidad there is a big local tradition called a "Camp". It usually was for youth and at the end of it, the tradition said that one could let go and have some fun, at someone else's expense of course. I knew this and at our orientations was very clear as to the difference between the camp and the institute and that the end of camp behavior was not acceptable at an institute, especially here in my home. However, at one of them, one of the boys who had been sent to this institute by someone else got the other boys together for a trick on the girls.

The girls all slept in the back room on mattresses on the floor. As we lived right next to the sea, the boys had been able to fill a large canvas bag with crabs! In the middle of the last night the boys released the crabs and sent them toward the back of the house. I was awakened by loud and shrill screams from the girls in the back room. The crabs were crawling all over them.

I was furious! I got everybody up but was so upset that I couldn't deal with them then. Lorna Bergner who was a visiting Ruhi Coordinator and tutor finished the institute with them before the sun came up. When I got up, I shared with them my disappointment and dismay at the disrespect I felt they had showed towards me and my family at our home. I had them pack their things and wait on the porch until their rides home came. I hope I did make it clear I was speaking to the boys, not the girls.

One of the better ones was an institute where everyone studied hard and clever skits were made up by groups at the end relating to the material we had just studied.

One group started out with two boys hanging out at the corner. One of the boys had his shirt unbuttoned several buttons, and his belt unbuckled. Bella Edoo who was another tutor for the institute was sitting next to me for this skit. She and I looked at each other, with our eyebrows raised.

The skit continues with two of girls who are supposed to be teaching the Faith in the area pass by. They stop and proceed to give the boys a Bahá'í fireside. The boys nod but it's clear they are not overly impressed. So the girls politely say goodbye and start to leave. As they turn around and walk away, one of them says to them in this silky tone of voice, "Oh baby, don't move away so fast".

At this point Bella and I both lost it, we could not stop laughing. It was so unexpected and so out of character for these boys it was really funny.

This is the group for that Institute.

L to R: Bella Edoo, Pat Paccassi, Kevin Brisport, Christopher Rooplal, Kimraj Badree, Joanna Greenidge, Mary Greenidge, Dwayne Burris. Dwight Burris, Shoba Maharaj.

It was at this institute that the Burris twins, Dwight and Dwaine, first became involved with the institute activities of the Faith. Their Father, Stephen was one of the Burris family who were early believers in Tobago, with their Mother being a Christian. The family did have the children involved in both religious activities. These included Christian Sunday School and the Bahá'í Feasts, Holy Day celebrations and etc.

As the boys were now 15, I kept after Stephen to have the boys come to this institute. Dhanika, their younger sister, being just 10 years of age, was not eligible to attend. She, being put out by this, solved her dilemma by telephoning the house at least twice a day during our break times. At some other time, she faced her Mother, who was not a Bahá'í on the subject of religion by saying to her, "Ms. Burris, you can send me to Sunday school all you want, but I am a Bahá'í."

I'm sure getting the boys to attend wasn't easy as this was also the time of a big sports event and they were great fans. However, one way or the other, they came. Within a day or two, the boys began to say things about the Faith such as "Well we should do that." or other similar remarks indicating they now were identifying themselves as Bahá'ís. At the end of the institute and the subsequent teaching project in a nearby village, one of the boys was heard to remark "I can't believe I didn't even miss TV!"

So many lessons other than the required syllabus were learned at the institutes. One of the times there was a young man invited who as it turned out was nowhere near the reading level it was felt was necessary to do these courses. There was a little grumbling about the slower pace we now had to go at. But he was here so I had him sit next to me the whole time and traced the words being read with my finger. Day by day his reading improved. By the end of the 9 days, his reading level had increased by at least 3 levels. His spiritual insights however were amazing. The grumbling stopped and he was getting lots of help.

Another time it had to do with music. Classical music was not the norm in the West Indies. It was my habit to play classical music in the morning. I continued to do so even at the institutes. It would play softly through the morning routine until it was time to start the prayers when I would then turn it off. One morning I was starting to put the music on when I noticed two of the girls sitting on the couch near me. I told them I was going to play the classical music now. Yes, they said, we have come to listen.

At the same institute one of the boys became really interested in the music as well and asked questions about it. I ended up playing Beethoven's Ninth Symphony all the way though and he stayed listening all the way.

One of the most popular extra activities that we did at one of the institutes was a skit entitled "Wizard of Justice". It was an adaption of the movie "Wizard of Oz" with the slant being Bahá'í and the characters having to get to the Universal House of Justice for advice.

But the same theme and characters were used. We dressed up in costumes as well as we could and really got into it. I was the wicked witch of the West. (Me melting in the photo) I have never minded making a fool of myself and really hammed up this part. The kids loved it, they screamed and clapped and laughed.

A great meeting was held in this house at the occasion of the visit of our spiritual Mother, Maxine Roth. The photo is us being silly. We wanted the gathering to be a fun time, so Maxine put together a game they had done at her pioneering post in Venezuela. There were families with three persons, a papa, momma and baby with all the last names sounding very similar; EG: Bissle, Fizzle, Dizzle, Mizzle, you get the idea.

Small pieces of paper were made for the name in each complete family IE: papa Bissle, momma Bissle, baby Bissle. Everyone was asked to pick a paper out of a bowl and find their family. So here are lots of Bahá'ís moving around talking to everyone trying to complete their family. When they did find each other they were to be seated in this order; Papa, Mama, Baby.

We announced the prizes for the first three complete families; third prize was you didn't have to stay and help clean up, second prize was you didn't have to help do the dishes afterwards, first prize was you got to pick who did clean up and do the dishes!!

TRINIDAD AND TOBAGO | 97

The winners:

At the institutes we also made an attempt to finish them with an activity relevant to the course. One of the ways was to do a small teaching trip into a nearby village. We would call upon the believers in the area and have the kids practice the parts of the course where one is out teaching. It also included sometimes putting up a display and talking to people who would stop and chat with us.

We also went to a nearby ongoing children's class and have our newly trained tutors give the class from Book 3. The children in these classes had, of course done, this material many times with other new trainees but they were always patient and polite.

Some of the special other activities that we did in Trinidad included a Walk in the village part of La Romain which was the Local Spiritual Assembly area we lived in. One time we planned a big event and asked the Bahá'ís from everywhere to join us. We started at one end of the village, La Romain. We walked all the way through carrying signs and plaques and also brought a steel pan for one of the men to play while we were there.

It was lots of fun. Probably didn't result into any new Bahá'ís but everyone sure got to know we were there. The following photos reflect the scope and support we got.

One night after a meeting at the house some of the Bahá'ís lingered, and we got talking about the musical talent in the Bahá'í community. As the conversation continued, we began to realize we could start a group that would showcase these divergent talents. The idea grew and was eventually brought together by one of the Trinidadian believers, Rhonda Holder (now Lewis). She became the director and one of the main stars as she had a beautiful singing voice. As there were varied talents in the group such as violin solos, dramatic readings, skits and a singing choir, it was called the Bahá'í Performing Theater.

This group met every Saturday at the Bahá'í Centre in the South of Trinidad. As there were members from North, this required traveling back and forth for them. But every Saturday, everyone showed up. It was not only a very talented group, but loving and united as well. The youngest member was a child named Ellie Rooplal. She was included as a voice like hers was not to be turned down no matter how old she was.

The group got really good, with a varied program and somehow, we managed to get outfits for everyone. There was no funding available other than what we all tried to raise. We had T-Shirts printed and we sold those. I even took a bunch back to the United States on one of my visits and sold them there. It got to be known up there as the Bahá'í Hamburger-T-Shirts as the design did, indeed, if one thought about it, look like there was a hamburger in the middle of the shirt.

We finally felt confident enough to start with public performances at other local centres. The first one was held at the Creative Arts Centre in San Fernando. We invited the whole Bahá'í community and asked them to bring their friends. The house was packed, and it turned out to be a very receptive audience. Stephen Burris and I acted as the hosts for the night. We gave a short introduction about the history of the group and what people should expect to see and hear for the evening. We also must have looked a bit strange. Stephen is quite tall, and quite dark. I am quite short and quite white. He wore a white outfit including our hamburger T-Shirt and white pants. I wore a black hamburger T-Shirt and black pants. We thought we looked lovely and hoped the intended contrasts were noted.

The nerves and jitters we all felt before it started vanished as the curtain rose. They were great, it all went smoothly. It was a real success! Boy, were we happy!! It was filmed and a copy remains and is on YouTube: https://youtu.be/qRHppEoiGC8.

Another public performance we gave was at the University of the West Indies. We used their large auditorium, sent out invitations, put up posters, and hoped for the best. We were once again very pleased with the turn out and the reception of the audience.

I began to have visions of them getting good enough to think about traveling as a group to other Bahá'í communities as a way of attracting larger audiences to Bahá'í activities. Unfortunately, this was not to be. It wasn't too long after the performance at the University that the group was made into a National Bahá'í Committee. Its leadership also changed, and it did not survive all the changes. But it was sure fun while it lasted.

Another change for me in Trinidad was that there were three Bahá'í Centres in the country. The National Bahá'í Centre was in Port of Spain in the North.

The Bahá'í Centre for South was in Palmyra. This centre served the surrounding Bahá'í communities and the land had been donated by Dr. Harry Collymore.

The Centre was used a great deal. The events and/or sessions were always well attended.

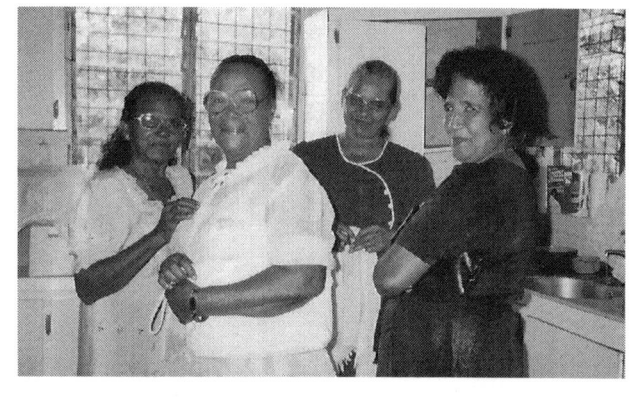

This is a photo of some of the lovely Bahá'ís in the Palmara area: L to R: ____, Merle Wilshire, ____, Jaitun Abdul.

The other Centre was in Paharry, which is in the North East of the country. It was this Centre where I had first begun to work actively for the Faith in Trinidad. Its caretakers were Dollie and Ramkay Ramjattan. Ramkay was a devoted and active Bahá'í. Every day he would pack up his Bahá'í materials and take off to teach the Faith in the area. He would touch each house and if there was an interest, he would teach them the Faith. If there was no interest, he went to the next house. This was a man I wanted to work with. Frank and I would drive the long drive, stay several days, go out with Ramkay during the day and have meetings at night.

One of the most touching things I can remember about working at this Centre had to do with a young boy, not quite in his teens yet. His home life was awful. He attended a meeting or two. I then invited him to come to one of the residential institutes we held there. His reading level was very low, and he had a lot of trouble memorizing anything. But after the night session I would work with him to memorize the prayer "Is there any Remover of Difficulties save God". It took the entire nine days he was there to accomplish this, but we were both very happy when he did learn it. A few years later I saw him once again, he ran up to me and said the whole prayer! God is good.

Trinidad is one part of a two-part nation. The second part is the island of Tobago which in my estimation, is more like what I think of as a Caribbean island. That is, it is not as commercially developed as Trinidad. The pace is slower, so there is more time to chat and relax. The first Bahá'í on either island was Shelia Burris. Peter McLaren came there on a teaching trip. He asked the taxi driver to take him to a place that was hard to get to. He made this request as it had been his experience as well as other Bahá'í teachers, was that the further one got from the capital, the more likely one could find those interested in religion. He was then taken to a village called Parlatuvier which, indeed, was a long way, by island standards, from the capital of Scarborough. He saw this young girl on the road and had the driver stop. He introduced himself, began telling her about the Faith. She was very interested, accepted the Faith and brought him to her home. The father was also very receptive, accepted the Faith and told his family to do the same which they did. Many of the family have remained steadfast as well as some of their next generation.

The Bahá'í community in Tobago is smaller, but just as devoted as the one in Trinidad. Our Institute Board decided to hold a weekend institute and asked Kathy Farabi and I to go and tutor the day-time sessions.

We were housed in a comfortable house that was not near any other houses. This helped with the ambience needed for study and concentration. However it also meant at night the two of us were pretty isolated. One night after everyone had left and we were sitting on the porch, a voice came from nowhere it seemed, saying "Good Night". We looked and there stood a man neither of us knew.

We probably both held our breath for a second until he said he had been invited to the meeting but had to work and could he come now. Going back to my experience on my global trip about trusting one's instincts and inner guidance, I thought for a minute, felt no sign of danger and said "Sure, come in." Kathy gave a start but didn't say anything, so he came onto the porch. We ended up having a really productive time with him. It was, once again, where one has to trust one's own instinct and guidance. It is, after all, one of the things we say prayers for but it's not an easy lesson to learn.

Two of the nicest compliments I ever received came from this island. One was after a nine-day institute. We were doing the normal wrap up with the whole group. Bobby who was one of the other tutors and the Auxiliary Board Member said to the group "We have been here in their home for 9 days, this is their home, not a Bahá'í Centre, and yet not once have they made us feel uncomfortable".

The other came from one of the older youth Navid Lancaster. One day we were sitting on my porch chatting. He asked me about pioneering. One of the things I said was that the only thing I regretted was that I had not been able to see my grandsons who lived in the United Sates, grow up. He looked at me, put his hand on his heart and said, "I am one of your grandsons."

Two more very fond memories happened the night we left Trinidad. Bella Edoo, who was married to Ashmeed and now one of my dearest friends, asked if she could have a going away party for us. I agreed but with the condition that no "going away speeches" be given. Lynn, Frank and I finished the last of the packing just after dark. We had to hurry to the Bahá'í Centre in Palmyra as this was where the gathering was being held. We drove up and the Centre parking area was full and overflowing. The national Bahá'í community had come! I was so touched and for once didn't know what to say.

For that night, the youth had planned a surprise for me. They had resurrected the "Wizard of Justice" skit as a going away performance for me. They looked fantastic, they were all in appropriate costumes, and the Tin Man was even wrapped completely in tin foil!

Just as the party was winding up, I went outside and the youth followed me. We chatted a bit and when it came to say goodnight, one of the youth ran up and gave me a big hug. This triggered the others who immediately lined up for their hug. This still brings tears to my eyes when I think of it.

A word about our leaving Trinidad; this was not our choice. We wanted to stay and did everything we could think of to make it happen, including having a glowing recommendation from Dr. Collymore who was well known and respected in the nation. Frank especially made efforts which were not the norm. I usually took care of things like that, but one day, he even called the appropriate Minister of Government to intervene for us. It was not to be.

We were also unsure as to where to go. After exploring what seemed to be all the available options, we decided to return to St. Lucia where our permanent residency seemed to be still valid. Going backwards had never been our pattern but it was the only open option. We decided to make a test run, as our Permanent Resident status was still valid in our passports. We booked a flight to St. Lucia and had no trouble entering the country.

We then made all the arrangements, packing, shipping etc. and flew into the Vigie Airport in St. Lucia. We chose the Residents line as opposed to Visitors. We showed our passports to the Immigration Officer, who looked at them, turned to us, smiled and said, "Welcome home".

| 8 |

ST. LUCIA: 2000 TO PRESENT (MAY 2020)

I arrived in St. Lucia with mixed emotions. First, I really wanted to stay in Trinidad, but here we were in spite of all our efforts. I knew then that Bahá'u'lláh wanted us here, not in Trinidad any longer. It wasn't until I took a visit to Trinidad a few years later and attended a National Convention that I realized why we had to leave. I looked around and saw so many local Trinidadians in the forefront of the Bahá'í activities and administration that I knew that we weren't needed there for support anymore.

We first stayed at one of the Bahá'ís, Urmie Persaud's, house in Sunny Acres which is right outside of the capital Castries. We met with the National Spiritual Assembly and they asked us to move to Choiseul to help with the consolidation of the Faith in the area of La Fargue, Choiseul. A St. Lucian and member of the National Assembly, Conrad Dos Santos lived there, and it was felt we could him help with the work of the Faith.

He took us around the village helping us to find a house to live in. One of the last houses he took us to was owned by a friend of his who moved back and forth between the United States and here. It was a big house, 4 bedrooms, lots of space, and a lovely view of the sea. We were chatting on the back porch and I asked if I could look around the house. Calixte Joseph, the owner, looked a little startled but said "Sure". Frank and I liked it a lot and as we were leaving, I said to Calixte, "We would like to rent your house but can't afford a large rent". He looked at me strangely and said, "I don't want to rent my house".

Oops, it seems Conrad had taken us here to meet his friend, not as a possibility to rent his house.

Now I gulped, apologized but we then began to talk about the idea of our renting it as he was out of the country so much. We did come to an agreement and we stayed there for about two years.

It was in this house that we celebrated our 50th wedding anniversary on 15 October 2000. It was a wonderful gathering; all our family and friends from St. Lucia came as well as Bella and Ashmeed Edoo and Marlene Ramlal from Trinidad, and my sister Jill and niece Michele from the United States.

Frank and Conrad worked together every week contacting the Bahá'ís who were on our membership list. Everyone was cordial but did not attend the meetings they were invited to. At one time I visited four ladies with Conrad and invited them to study the Faith with us at our house. The day arrived as did the ladies. Conrad did not come. It was a matter of misunderstanding, Conrad thinking it was for ladies alone and the ladies really put off by Conrad not attending the meeting. This effectively stopped this gathering from happening again.

I was asked by the National Assembly to serve on the National Teaching Committee. I told them that I had many years' experience on the National Institute Board in Trinidad I would prefer to serve on the Board in St. Lucia as well. This was accepted and I began to work with the first Board shown below in the photo.

L to R; Moses Auguste, Verdia Louis, Urmie Persaud, Pat Paccassi

We had our first meeting, started to

elect officers and with four members we were in a deadlock with two votes for me as chairman and two votes for me as secretary. We paused and Urmie Persaud asked, "Doesn't the secretary do most of the work?" I replied "Yes" and the next vote I was elected secretary and Moses Auguste was chairman with Verdia Louis and Urmie as members. The Institute members did change but I stayed on as secretary until the Institute Board concept was changed when it was dissolved in 2009 with a new Caribbean Initiative Committee appointed and I was not on it.

The photo of another (2006) Institute Board:

L to R: Seated; Pat Paccassi, Grace Leonce

Standing; Moses Auguste, Ada Leonce, Betty Antoine-Faucher

I was able to share the idea of residential institutes and the first one was planned for July 2001. Once again as we lived in a big house, the nine-day institute was held there. At this time there were not enough trained tutors on St. Lucia to carry out this institute. I contacted Bella Edoo from Trinidad asking her to come and help. There was also a young travel teacher, Vahid Elliq, from the United States and he attended the institute as well. Their names are on the photo itself.

In 2001, the year following our return to St. Lucia, I was once again elected to the National Spiritual Assembly. This meant for me three hours traveling time to and from the National Assembly meetings.

As living in Trinidad was literally rent free for 10 years, we still had the bulk of the money left to Frank by first, his mother, and then after her death, his stepfather. After a lot of discussion, we finally decided to build a house for ourselves in this area. We had always lived in wooden houses in St. Lucia. They were built in Green Heart lumber from Guyana. This is a very strong and pretty wood and hard enough to, as the local saying goes, "Break the teeth of termites".

We looked around for a builder and decided on one whose price seemed more reasonable than others. Who we picked turned out to be a bad decision. He was a crook and ended up building only the outer frame of the house. He did buy much of what we needed for the inside such as, windows, etc., but left us with a useless signed contract and had spent all of the money but $5000. And this was the monies earmarked for "…finished-house" matters.

This was the condition of the house that he left us with.

Later we found out that we were not the first he cheated. I compiled a list of the others and built a case for fraud. The police came and said there probably wasn't anything they could do. Later, I found out that his mother was a Police Matron at one of the nearby women's prisons. His father had done the same thing before him and had fled the country.

Years later, I heard that he also had fled to Trinidad, started the same scheme, got caught, and there he was sent to prison.

We did find another builder and was able to finish the house in 2003 and I still live here. There is a lovely view including the Caribbean Sea, a large mango tree and swaying coconut trees. I happily meditate and say my prayers each morning enjoying the quiet and safety of the area of La Fargue, Choiseul in which we built our house. As the Rasta's say here "Jah provides."

One of the courses that I wanted to hold here that was not a Ruhi course was one that our friend, Erica Toussaint, put together and held in Portland, Oregon. It was on the Bahá'í covenant and her description of the two-day course and the response to it intrigued me. I wanted to hold it here. I invited a few of the more deepened Bahá'ís and it was held at the Bahá'í Centre in Castries. The idea was to cover the Will and Testament of 'Abdu'l-Bahá and give some emphasis to the work and lives of the Hands of the Cause of God. To enhance this course, photos of all of the Hands were posted for the second day. We were surrounded by them and the effect was startling. We were looking at a group of people whose services to the Faith were unique.

At one point, we were talking about Charles Mason Remy and his claim to be the second Guardian. A young St. Lucian Bahá'í, Moses Auguste, stood up, threw his pencil down and exclaimed "Good God, couldn't the man read?"

This same course was also well received in Trinidad and Barbados.

The Ruhi Institutes continued, with both an intensive residential institute and later a weekly one in my home.

This first photo is an early 9 day residential one held in Augier:

These later ones were held weekly at my house.

We had designed an Award Certificate of Participation listing the book completed and gathered the participants for Award Ceremonies.

These awards were really welcomed in this country. Recognition of efforts and accomplishments here are not the norm. I have had Bahá'ís years later ask for a duplicate certificate as the one they were given had become damaged.

I have included these several examples to show the extent of the efforts made on behalf of the Institute Process in St. Lucia. The Core Activities were held and promoted in the whole island. It has been my great pleasure and honour to serve it.

Efforts were not only in St. Lucia. In 2005 the Continental Board of Counsellors held a Conference for the Caribbean in Antigua.

A Message from the Universal House of Justice to the conference outlined its purpose;

> "..In presenting to you the features of the coming Five Year Plan, the subject of your deliberations in this conference, we will review the record of recent accomplishments of the Bahá'í world and indicate how current approaches, methods and instruments should be carried to this next stage."

Representatives from all our islands attended, including the wider islands and area of the Caribbean. We met, shared, learned and returned to our countries determined to further the Institute process. I was especially happy to see Bella and Ashmeed Edoo from Trinidad. Bella came up to me and we hugged and hugged and hugged. It had been so long since we had seen one another. One of the friends watching later said "That was the longest hug I've ever seen"

In 2006 when I was 78 years old, I asked the National Assembly permission and blessing to retire from service at the National Spiritual Assembly level. It was given and my life at that point underwent an unexpected dramatic change. I was no longer "in the loop" so to speak. We were living in an area a good distance from an active Bahá'í community and the area in which we live no longer seemed to be interested in hearing anything about the Bahá'í Faith. We were well treated here in La Fargue with concern and lots of help from those around us. They like us but are not interested in our religion.

The years had settled into a pattern of being Bahá'ís in the South West area of the island. Most of the other Bahá'ís lived in the north of the island, which by island standards, was a long distance from us. Visitors and Bahá'ís from there would come once in a while to visit, and everyone told us it was a "long drive". Timewise, it took one and a half hours one way.

In 2010 we celebrated our 60th Wedding Anniversary. It was a big celebration. Our friends and family came to share this moment with us. I always said of our time together that we were "happily" married all those years! I cannot imagine a better husband than Frank Paccassi.

This photo was taken at our 60th wedding anniversary right after we had said our Bahá'í vows. As we had become Bahá'ís way after we were married, we thought it would be nice to say the Bahá'í marriage vows on our anniversary with all our friends and family present.

We spent our time in La Fargue pretty much settled into a routine that now suited our advancing years. It was not strenuous but steady. We saw the Bahá'í friends as much as possible; told people about the Bahá'í Faith as much as possible and took care of every-day chores as best we could. I always felt that all was well when we were together.

Then on the 5 December 2017 it all changed. I was sitting on the porch in the morning, saying my prayers as usual. But now in my view were several people chatting on the road in front of me. They had stopped and were showing no signs of moving. I became annoyed and decided to move inside to finish my prayers in peace.

Frank had made our yogurt breakfast drink as usual. He was eating at the dining room table which in our house is one open-room area of living, dining and kitchen. He was sitting right behind me at the table. I heard a noise that sounded like a rattle. I turned around and thought Frank looked strange. I asked him if he was ok. He didn't answer so I got up and went over to him. As I got there, I caught him just as he started to fall out of his chair. I wasn't really alarmed then as he had fainted a few times before. I held him like that for 10 minutes, and now suspected he was gone. I stayed liked that for a half hour. He was gone. I then leaned way over and got a pillow from one of the chairs, placed it on the table and carefully laid his precious head on it. He was 89 years old.

He was buried 9 days later with a lovely Bahá'í program in a lovely area in La Tourney Cemetery. We had a "two" compartment tomb built and I shall be buried there as well. It seems only right as we always wanted to be together.

An email was sent to the Universal House of Justice informing them. They returned one calling him an "...illumined soul" as well as other endearing and heartwarming remarks. Others came as well from the International Teaching Centre and the National Spiritual Assembly of the Bahá'ís of the United States.

The following year on 3 June 2018 I had my 90th birthday party sharing with many friends and lots of food. Bella came from Trinidad for the weekend before bringing and sending presents for the day itself. One was a crown and when I asked her about it, she said "You are the queen for the day"! It's not every day you turn 90."

At the end of summer in 2018, it was nice to be asked to give the closing talk at the Youth Camp held near me at the Balenbouche Estate. The youth are lovely, and I always enjoy being with them. They are so sincere and our future as well.

In looking back over the years I realize that so many things I have done and been part of could never have been accomplished were I not a Bahá'í. There is nothing in my background or training to qualify me to do what I have been able to do while serving the Faith. It has been a distinct honour and privilege and I am very grateful for the opportunities given to me. There is always someone with me Monday to Friday during the day. I am still strong enough to be by myself at night and on the weekends with pretty much the same routine. As my memory is still good, I decided to finish these "recollections" which I had started years ago. I am not at all sure if they are of any value, but it gives me something to do and perhaps a future historian will be happy I did them. One can only hope!

'YÁ BAHÁ'U'L-ABHÁ'

"O Glory of the All-Glorious"

| 9 |

STORIES:
HANDS OF THE CAUSE OF GOD STORIES

Being in the right place at the right time! These recollections which I choose to share are ones which could have happened only at a special time in history.

AMATU'L-BAHÁ RÚHÍYYIH KHÁNUM

My first encounter with Rúhíyyih Khánum was in St. Thomas in 1970 when she and Violette Nakhjavání came for a visit.

We knew, of course, who she was, but it does not prepare one for the force of both her personality and depth. There was something about her that I could not put my finger on. After she left, I thought about it a lot, and three months later it suddenly dawned on me, she displayed the quality of majesty. No wonder I didn't recognize it, I had never seen it manifested before.

However there was another side to her that anyone who has spent any time with her at all will agree, she could use a very open, blunt way of expressing her opinion.

During this trip she visited our home. The area where we did all our entertaining and visiting was on the second floor. At the top of the stairs was a large painting of 'Abdu'l-Bahá that had been painted for us by a dear friend. She stopped in her tracks as she saw it, turned to me and said, "Burn it, there isn't an artist alive who can properly paint the essence of Abdu'l-Baha". Wow! As I was a fairly new Bahá'í and didn't know one was supposed to keep ones opinion to themselves when around her, and just say "Yes Ma'am", I started to give her arguments as to why I shouldn't do that. My closing and final point which I thought was the clincher was "…but Rúhíyyih Khánum, this was done for us in love". She looked at me with a look mixed with annoyance and impatience, and said "Pat, people commit murder for love".

I did take it down as long as she was there but could not bring myself to burn it.

When she left St. Thomas, I could hear my heart breaking. I can still see myself standing at the airport watching her go. She suddenly turned around, saw the look on my face, and came back to me, saying "Oh Pat". Then with a look of both annoyance and affection on her face leaned down and gave me a kiss on both cheeks.

She visited Barbados in 1972 where we had moved as pioneers. We asked her to dinner and she and Violette graciously consented. As she walked into the house, she saw an abstract painting hanging on the wall, stopped, looked at me and said "Pat, did you have this in St. Thomas?" I said, "Yes Ma'am, you didn't like it there either". She burst out laughing, I gathered not many people talked to her like that, and thank God, she was not displeased with me.

In 1978, I was privileged to attend the Five-Day International Convention in Haifa Israel, along with hundreds of other delegates from around the world.

One day, I woke up so sick I could not get out of bed. I was devastated! How could I miss even one of the five precious days, but nevertheless, I could not get out of bed. So I stayed and prayed and prayed and prayed.

Suddenly an idea came to me, I wondered if I could, somehow, get to Rúhíyyih Khánum and ask her for prayers or something! But it didn't take long for me to realize how impossible that was. Ah, but another idea came, I bet if I could somehow get hold of Violette Nakhjavání, surely she could get to Rúhíyyih Khánum for me. It also didn't take a lot of time for me to realize that wasn't going to happen either. So, back to praying.

The next day I woke and was well! I was able to attend the sessions for that day. During a lull in one of the meetings, I got up and wandered into one of the halls and stood there all by myself. I look up and there, coming up the hall, was Rúhíyyih Khánum, all by herself. That stunned me, as I had never, ever, seen her alone at an International Convention. I knew her from her visits to the West Indies and had the great honour to take her to media interviews, etc., as well as having her to my home. As she passed, she nodded, saying, "How are you? I responded with "I'm fine." She stopped dead in her tracks, looked at me and said with an emphatic tone as only she could, "I asked you how you were" Oops, I remembered my previous day's wish and replied, "Much better Khánum, thank you!". She nodded and went on her way.

After this session was over, I was leaving, and up the corridor strides Rúhíyyih Khánum, Violette Nakhjavání and the usual crowd of those around her. As Violette spotted me, and without missing a step, says to her "Khánum, you remember Pat, don't you?" Khánum turned to her, without missing a step either says, "Of course I remember her, I saw her earlier."

Wow, the Holy Land, both of my heartfelt wishes granted!

ABU'L-QÁSIM FAIZI

When I took my Pilgrimage in 1972 and combined it with a teaching trip around the world, and knowing that I would be traveling in India, one person that I really wanted to meet was Mr. Faizi. There had been several Hands who had traveled in the Caribbean, but not he. As I was a fairly new Bahá'í, this was a new feeling, unexplained, but strong.

Alas, as I traveled through India, when I was in the north of the country, he was in the south; when I traveled south, he moved to the north. It was one of only two disappointments during my whole trip in what was an incredible time for me. So, I told myself, Patricia, don't complain!

The following year, 1973, was the year of the Bahá'í International Convention. Frank and I were both on the National Assembly and thus accorded the wonderful bounty of attending as delegates. My wild story on how we got the money to attend I've already told in the Barbados chapter.

One day after a session on Mount Carmel, a group of us were standing in front of the entrance to the Shrine of the Báb, trying to decide where to have dinner. As we chatted, we saw a long limousine pull up, the driver's door opens and out jumps Ian Semple, a member of the Universal House of Justice, who runs around and opens the door of the limousine. As we watch with open mouths several Hands of the Cause of God get out of the car! But they are practically running towards the entrance to the Shrine, not stopping, not looking sideways, just straight ahead.

As the last Hand jumps out, I see its Mr. Faizi. Oh my, my heart starts to pound. As he reaches the entrance he stops, lifts his head up for a minute, and then walks straight over to me, takes my hand in his two hands, and says "My name is Faizi". Not another word is spoken; he turns and continues to walk into the Pilgrim House with the other Hands for their unscheduled visit with the Bahá'ís. He had heard my heart!

RAHMATU'LLÁH MUHÁJIR

During the visit of Dr. Muhájir in 1972 to Barbados, I was in the throes of deciding if I wanted to or could make the Pilgrimage to Israel that I had applied for only months ago.

After hearing this, He then proceeded to turn my life around by insisting that in connection with my Pilgrimage, I should make a teaching trip around the World.

This is not the forum for the resulting stories of my Global Teaching Trip. Joyce Olinga has made a DVD containing all of the stories from this trip. She has done an amazing job both of editing and including photos. It can be obtained from her web site. Her remarks re: this DVD entitled "Pat Paccassi's Incredible 1972 Global Travel Teaching Trip" are as follows:

"As many of you know Pat Paccassi is a long-time pioneer and a dear friend from my years of pioneering in the Caribbean. In 2011, it was my honor to video tape Pat during my visit to St. Lucia as she wanted to leave something for her family and Baha'is there. Once I began to edit, I became so inspired and moved that I felt compelled to make it a documentary available for the whole world. Thus, her interview is tightly edited with photos from her life and journey, photos of my trips to Uganda and the Caribbean as well as other contributors. This video shares a glimpse of what it was like to pioneer and travel-teach in the 70's.

The documentary has now successfully passed the U.S. Baha'i Reviewing Committee and can be offered for sale for $15, including US shipping from Olinga Productions, P.O. Box 14232, Maryland Heights, MO 63043.

Pat delightfully shares her early pioneering days and incredible journey to 14 countries with her unique sense of humor, boundless faith, unwavering courage and love of Bahá'u'lláh.

Baha'is throughout the Caribbean and many parts of the world will get to see many sites and gatherings including priceless photos of the Houses of The Báb and Bahá'u'lláh. In addition, Mrs. Paccassi, like Bahá'í pioneers in the 1970's, was blessed with having personal experiences and guidance from Hands of the Cause of God.

How grateful I am to have produced this precious glimpse of our Bahá'í history and may it inspire you as well to share the Glad Tidings that the Promised One has come!

With Caribbean waves of love and happiness,"

Joyce Olinga
OlingaProductions@mac.com

JOHN ROBARTS

In 1980, St. Lucia had the pleasure of a visit from John and Audrey Robarts. They were such a delightful couple, he with his stories and laughter and she with her laughter and support of him. During this time frame Mr. Robart's memory loss was becoming apparent. He would be telling a wonderful story and forget some detail or a name and he would look at her and she immediately provided what he needed.

Later in talking to her by herself, she said that she really had to pay attention during his stories, even though she had heard them many times, as she never knew when he was going to need a detail.

During this visit, he insisted on taking both the Bloodworth family, Keith, Stephanie, and their boys Ruhi and Badi, Canadian pioneers, and our family, the Paccassis, me, Frank and our youngest daughter, Judy out to dinner. No matter what we said, he said he wanted to do that for us as he understood we probably didn't go out to dinner very often.

One night I cooked a big dinner and went to pick them up at their hotel. He asked where we were going that night for dinner, and I replied I know a nice Italian place. "Great he said, I love Italian food". So when I drove up into our driveway, he got it! They both had a good laugh and more importantly enjoyed their Italian dinner. Audrey even asked me how I knew green split pea soup was John's favorite, and I replied it was one of mine as well, and cooks always make what they like to eat!

COLLIS FEATHERSTONE

In 1984, St. Lucia had the distinct pleasure of having Mr. and Mrs. Collis Featherstone be present for the National Convention. He was also at the groundbreaking ceremony of the National Centre property on the Morne which was a lovely site overlooking the sea and the capital Castries.

Frank and I were the lucky pioneers who picked them up at the airport and took them to their hotel. We sat chatting for a while, and I then informed them of their schedule on the island which included dinner at one of the pioneer family's home, the Babahanis', that evening.

Mr. Featherstone then began to speak as to how wonderful and gracious it was of the pioneers who, in spite of their busy full lives of home, family and Bahá'í duties take the time to have them to dinner. I sat listening to this with growing impatience. When he was finished, I said to him, "Mr. Featherstone, you know full well that the pioneers flip each other to see who gets to have you for dinner"

They both burst out laughing. They knew it was true!

PAT'S MISCELLANEOUS STORIES

LEARNING A NEW CULTURE

I am not going to even attempt to go very deeply into this subject, but a few prime examples do come to mind that I think pretty much explain some of a pioneer's experiences. The first two were in the 1980's, so a lot of that has changed.

1. Keith and Stephanie Bloodworth and their infant son, Ruhi, first came to St. Lucia in 1978 to pioneer. Being devoted and obedient servants of the Faith, they soon moved to the village of Dennery that needed help.

They lived in a house on the beach and on the main street. They had no stove so cooked everything on a coal pot. Keith had by this time obtained a job teaching Art in the Secondary School in Castries, the capital city. It was about an hour's bus drive to his school, and classes started at 8.00 am. That meant that Stephanie rose every morning at 4.30 am to start preparing breakfast and his lunch to take to school.

Steph bought some groceries as most did, in a small shop on the main street. Soon after they got there, Stephanie went to buy a few things in the shop. She asked for a dozen eggs and the shocked clerk said, "Oh no, Miss, I can't sell one person that many eggs!" A small shop carried only a small of amount of anything most of the time. Most people, knowing this bought exactly the number of eggs that were needed at the moment. Stephanie said all right, give me what you can, and I will also take a pound of cheese. The clerk stopped, swirled her eyes to one side, thought about that for a bit, and then with an incredulous look said "Miss, that's 16 ounces!" The quantity of what one bought at a time applied to the cheese as well!

2. Back in the old days when I was still smoking, I was in Grenada on a teaching trip. We were in a village with its shop on the main street. I went in and asked the man for a carton of cigarettes. He looked at me, and said "Oh Miss, sorry, I don't sell wholesale." Later I found out that most people bought one or, at the most, two cigarettes at a time.

HAIFA

During a trip to Haifa, Israel for my second Pilgrimage in 2004, I was standing in one of the meeting halls waiting to go to the next scheduled event.

While there, a young Persian man came moving very quickly by me, skidded to a stop, and said to me "I am taking some people to the next meeting in my car, would you like to come with us? I, of course, was delighted, being long past my high energy ability to walk up high hills, and I replied in my most polite manner, "I wouldn't mind". He looked at me, hesitated and then repeated exactly what he had asked me in the first place, only in a slower, louder tone of voice. I realized what had just happened; he had not understood the idiom. I then said, in my most polite manner, "That would be very nice, thank you, I would like a ride." He beamed and proceeded to give me directions where to meet him.

MAMIE SETO

In 1953, Mamie Seto, a long time Bahá'í was a member of the National Spiritual Assembly of the Bahá'ís of the United States. In the opening of the World Crusade (1953-1963) the Guardian issued a call to pioneering. She was one of the five members who resigned from the National Spiritual Assembly and went to a pioneering post. Mrs. Seto went to Japan.

I first became aware of her when she came to Sacramento, California in 1964 to speak at a meeting sponsored by the local spiritual assembly. To the best of my knowledge I could not have done anything other than say hello, as it was a large gathering and I was a new Bahá'í. Actually, I don't even remember saying that.

The following year, our family was at Bahá'í Summer School at Geyserville, California. I was sitting with a gathering listening to one of the talks being given under the wonderful, large tree that was its hallmark feature.

My first-born daughter, Lynn, who had been out playing with the other children, came up to me quietly and said "Mom, a lady wants to talk to you." I said "OK, but not now honey, I am listening to this talk" She in turn, who was normally a well behaved and obedient child kept insisting that I come "Now" as the lady said to her "Child, go get your Mother" and she also said "Now". By this time, the whispered conversation I was having with Lynn was beginning to penetrate the Bahá'ís near me, and with them looking at us, I said, alright and got up to follow Lynn to the lady.

As I went across the all but empty field, I could see a woman sitting in a chair all by herself. As I got closer, I could see it was Mamie Seto! I went up to her and said "Mrs. Seto, you wanted to see me?" She looked up, looked straight in my eyes and said, "I want you to go pioneering!" I was really taken back, but as Frank and I had already made that decision ourselves, I told her that. She nodded, said "Good" and put her head back down, with nothing more to say.

In the next months, our efforts to go pioneering seemed to be stymied. Frank, with an engineering background and experience, had sent many resumes looking for a job. There were no replies. During that period we again went to Geyserville to hear Hand of the Cause of God, Bill Sears speak.

As one might expect, considering the esteem the Bahá'ís hold for a Hand of the Cause, the meeting hall was packed. His talk had already started; we were sitting near the back. Our row began to shuffle a bit to allow someone who had arrived late to take a seat at the far end of the row. As she passed me, I saw it was Mamie Seto. She didn't look at me, continued to her seat, but then leaned forward, somehow knowing I was still looking at her, and she said, "You're still here". I whisper back, "We are going!" She nodded and our conversation was once again terminated.

Not too long after, in October 1965, our pioneering wishes were granted. We went first to Puerto Rico. Frank got a job and lost it. The Foreign Goals Committee said to try St. Thomas as they were to form the first National Spiritual Assembly of the Bahá'ís of the Leeward, Windward and Virgin Islands. Frank did get a job there and we moved in July 1966.

In October 1967, Six Intercontinental Conferences were called by the Universal House of Justice, the closest to us was being held was in Chicago, Illinois. We were privileged to attend.

During a break in the sessions, we were standing in one of the corridors. I looked up to see the Bahá'ís parting as if it were the Red Sea and in the middle walking towards us was Mamie Seto! I was astounded! As she got to me, she stopped, looked at me, and said "You're back", I said "Oh no, Mrs. Seto, we are just here for the Conference". She nodded, said "Good", gave me kiss on the cheek and was on her way!!

A few years later, one night I awoke from a sound sleep, thinking "Mamie Seto is dying". One of my friends in the States who knew of my earlier encounters with Mrs. Seto contacted me with the same sad information. I only replied, "I heard".

I swear, that is the complete conversations I had with Mrs. Seto. How did she know? What a wonderful and mysterious religion we belong to. We have guardian angels, who for the most part, we don't even know about. God is good!

TWO UNEXPECTED EVENTS ON PILGRIMAGE

In 1972 I was most fortunate to be able to go on Pilgrimage to the Holy Land and visit the Bahá'í Holy Shrines in Israel. Our family was pioneering in Barbados at that time.

In those earlier days if one applied from somewhere other than a large country, one could expect to go in a relatively short time. This was, I suppose, because of the smaller number of Bahá'ís who applied from around the world, and a wider representation of more countries attending was desirable.

At any rate, within months of applying, I was there. This too, is a good story, but for another day.

When I was a new Bahá'í in Carmichael, California in 1964, I was often dismayed at the laxity that Bahá'ís took to showing up at events on time. I have always been time orientated, so this bothered me, but I was told, "Oh, don't worry, this is Bahá'í time".

During the Pilgrimage, a visit to meet with the members of the Universal House of Justice was scheduled for 4:00 pm on one of our first days. What a wonderful prospect! Our small group of Pilgrims gathered before time in the room where we were to meet them. We stood around, chatting a bit, and without noticeable intrusion, chairs began to appear, and the pilgrims were herded into them. The chatting stopped and we sat quietly for a bit, and then, an adjoining door to our room opened and out filed the members of the Universal House of Justice! It was truly one of the most thrilling moments of my life. I still feel the emotion well within me when I think of it. I looked up at the clock, it said 4.00pm. I thought: "Now, that is Bahá'í time."

They spoke to us, and afterwards they stayed and chatted with us. I noticed that most of the Bahá'ís had opened their prayer books, asking each member to sign them. I, of course, wanted to, but just couldn't make myself do it. It just didn't seem right. It was like they were movie stars or famous musicians or authors, and that was not how I felt about them. So, the moment passed, and my prayer book remained unsigned.

A few days later, I went to the larger house of 'Abdu'l-Bahá which was then being used as the meeting place for the Universal House of Justice and its staff. I was to have lunch with one of the staff that I had known before.

As I was waiting for her, Mr. Hushmand Fatheazam, a member of the Universal House of Justice, was just going out to lunch. I did not know him other than the brief meeting that the pilgrims had previously had. But as he saw me, he stopped and said, "Wait a minute, I have something for you". For me? He went back into his office and came out right away with a book in his hand. It was a copy of his book, the "The New Garden." I opened it and he had signed it and inscribed a short message to me which started with my name! Again, how do they do this; how do they know?

| 10 |

CURRICULUM VITAE
OF BAHÁ'Í EXPERIENCES

PIONEERING SERVICE FOR PAT PACCASSI

NAME: Mrs. Patricia June Paccassi
NATIONALITY: North American
COUNTRY OF DOMICILE: St. Lucia, West Indies
LANGUAGE: English
BIRTHDATE: 3 June 1928

- Enrollment, Carmichael, California, March 1964.

- Pioneering from October 1965 to present (May 2020), in the Eastern Caribbean Islands residing in Puerto Rico, St. Thomas, Virgin Islands, Barbados, St. Vincent, Dominica, St. Lucia, Trinidad, and again to St. Lucia.

- Served in most all aspects of Baha'i Committee structures.

- Served on Local Spiritual Assemblies in St. Thomas, Barbados, St. Lucia, and Trinidad.

- Have been travel teaching to most English-Speaking islands in the Eastern Caribbean.

- Coordinated Mass Teaching Projects in Barbados, St. Vincent, Grenada and St. Lucia.

- Coordinated National Spiritual Assemblies responsibilities for the

Regional Auxiliary Board Member Conference held in St. Lucia August 1984.

- Served on National Spiritual Assemblies in the Eastern Caribbean for 25 years, with officer responsibilities of Corresponding Secretary, Recording Secretary, and Chairman. I asked to be retired from this level of service in St. Lucia in 2006 at the age of 78.

- Attended as a delegate to International Baha'i Conventions in 1973, 1978, 1983, and 2003

- Attended 100th Commemoration of the passing of Bahá'u'lláh in the Holy Land as one of the 19 representatives from Trinidad and Tobago.

- In 1972, in conjunction with my Pilgrimage, I took a travel teaching trip around the world to Uganda, Iran, India, Burma, Thailand, Singapore, Philippine Islands, Hong Kong, Japan, and Hawaii.

- Travel Teaching with Meherangiz Munsiff in 1985 to Grenada, Trinidad and Tobago, Guyana, Suriname, Brazil, Uruguay, Paraguay, Argentina, Bolivia, Ecuador, Peru and Panama.

- Coordinated and conducted first annual Mona Project for Counsellors, July and August 1985 in Grenada.

- Conducted monthly deepening Ruhi Institutes for a year after arriving in Trinidad.

- Served as Assistant to the Auxiliary Board Member, Ganesh Ramsahai, for the area of Rio Claro, Trinidad.

- Appointed to first Board of Directors of the National Bahá'í Institute of Trinidad and Tobago serving as secretary. Received training in Institute Process at Ruhi Institute in Cali, Columbia.

- Travelled to the Leeward, Windward and Virgin Islands headquarters, collecting historical information on the growth of the Faith in their respective areas. Both audio and video interviews of long-time believers were made in each island. Additional material was gathered from the National Bahá'í Archives of the United States and Canada.

- Established web site putting the chronological listings of the Pioneers, Travel Teachers and Events to respective islands with photos, videos and stories on a Web site entitled "Bahá'í Faith in the Caribbean". The web address is www.bahaihistorycaribbean.info

- Appointed to Board of Directors of the National Bahá'í Institute Board of Directors of St. Lucia in 2000. Served as Secretary/Treasurer until 2009 when the Boards were replaced by the Caribbean Initiative.

- Conducted weekend course on the Covenant in Trinidad, Barbados, and St. Lucia.

- Non-Bahá'í involvement in St. Lucia: served as secretary on the St. Lucia National Council of Women's Voluntary Organizations.

- Received acknowledgment of volunteer work as one of the "25 Outstanding Women in St. Lucia" they honoured at their 25th Anniversary Awards Ceremony held at the Prime Ministers Official Residence in 2001.

PIONEERING SERVICE FOR FRANK PACCASSI

NAME: Frank Edward Paccassi
NATIONALITY: North American
COUNTRY OF DOMICILE: St. Lucia, West Indies
LANGUAGE: English
BIRTHDATE: 19 August 1928 (Deceased 5 December 2017 in St. Lucia)

- Enrollment, Carmichael, California, March 1964.

- Participated in First West Coast Teacher Training Institute, conducted by Mildred Mottahedeh for the National Teaching Committee, Fresno, California December 1964/January 1965.

- Pioneering from October 1965 to present, in the Eastern Caribbean residing in Puerto Rico, St. Thomas, Virgin Islands, Barbados, St. Vincent, Dominica, St. Lucia, Trinidad, and back to St. Lucia.

- Served in most all aspects of Baha'i committee structures.

- Served on local Spiritual Assemblies in Carmichael, California; St. Thomas; Barbados; St. Lucia; Trinidad.

- Participated in Mass Teaching Projects in Barbados and St. Lucia.

- Served on National Spiritual Assemblies in Eastern Caribbean 14 years, with officer responsibility of Treasurer and Vice Chairman.

- Delegate to International Conventions in 1973 and 1983.

- Pilgrimage, July 1976.

- Attended 100th Commemoration of the passing of Bahá'u'lláh in the Holy Land as one of the 19 representatives from Trinidad and Tobago.

- Non-Bahá'í involvement: served as a Math and Science teacher in the islands of Barbados, Dominica and St. Lucia. Years later many former students from the Morne Technical College in St. Lucia recognized him and introduced themselves as former students and praised him for his work with them.

AUTHOR'S NOTE

I would like to thank those friends and family members who encouraged me to see that my recollections of our time in the islands were read by others. Particularly my Grandson Sean for his editing help and John Kolstoe without whose help and support this would never have been published.

Also, please accept my apologies for the "fuzziness" of some of the photos. Over the years as I was taking photos of group gatherings and projects, it never, ever, occurred to me that I should be paying attention to any special quality of the photographs. As you see, many shots of the Bahá'is had to be taken from group photographs.

With loving Bahá'í greetings,
Pat